The
BRIDGE *of* BOMBERS

"YOU'LL REMEMBER," THE HELMSMAN WARNED, "OR I'LL
HAVE YOUR ARM TORN OFF."

The Bridge of Bombers   Frontispiece (Page 42)

The
BRIDGE *of* BOMBERS

By
TED COPP

Illustrated by
LEON GREGORI

GROSSET & DUNLAP
PUBLISHERS - NEW YORK

CONTENTS

The
BRIDGE *of* BOMBERS

I.

Meet Major Death

SUNLIGHT streamed through the window and dappled Commander Bennett's neat desk, it fell on the deeply tanned hands of the visitor who was scribbling down the Navy man's plan. An orderly entered and handed the commander a slip of paper.

"Show him right in," Commander Bennett said. He turned to his companion. "It's young Knight. Got everything straight?"

"Yes. I still don't like it, but it's your idea and you guarantee its success, so—" The visitor shrugged. "After all, this is a war, not a tea party."

"Right." The commander rose as the orderly ushered Steve Knight into the room and stretched out his hand. "It's great to see you, Steve."

"Thank you, sir. It's swell to see you again."

"A bit different from our last meeting, eh?" As Steve Knight shifted his lanky body, Commander Bennett turned to his other guest. "Major, this is Steven Knight, the young man I told you about. Steve, Major Jeff Sears is in charge of the bomber ferry to England."

"We prefer to call it the bridge of bombers," Major Sears laughed as he shook hands with the young American. "I've heard a lot about you, Knight."

"Thank you." Steve looked from one man to the other, then addressing Commander Bennett, he said, "I've done exactly what you told me to, and, as you'll see by their report, the school gave me a clean bill of health." He dropped the report on Bennett's desk. "Now—how soon can I be certified for the Navy's air school?"

"The last time Steve asked me that question," Commander Bennett informed Sears, "I told him that, despite my friendship with his family, I couldn't certify him because he was too impulsive and irresponsible. To prove I was wrong, he flew a Czech refugee down to her son's plantation in Honduras— in a two-place Luscombe, mind you. Not only that, but he got mixed up with a ghost, a red-headed Irishman with a Spanish-Irish name, a very unpleasant secret agent named von Rein, and a fabulous place called the Devil's Hand."

"Sounds interesting," observed Sears, smiling.

"And dangerous," the Navy man added dryly. "Steve was instrumental in capturing von Rein and breaking up his submarine base. As a result, I radioed him that I could use him and as soon as he had landed in the United States, I shipped him out for an intensive course in transport flying. Let's see how it turned out."

Picking up the report Commander Bennett studied it with growing interest. Sears and Steve Knight watched his expression as he read. The commander whistled softly and glanced at Sears.

"He's your man all right, Jeff. These people say that although he is still a few years too young to get a job as a transport pilot, they will recommend him very highly to any air line in the country."

"May I see it?" Sears asked.

Commander Bennett handed over the report and asked Steve:

"Would you be willing to postpone your entrance into naval aviation for a few months?"

"I've done everything you asked me to," Steve pointed out.

"I know, Steve, but this—well, the job I have in mind for you is a very special one. It will give you invaluable experience. More than that, you will be doing your bit to lift oppression from the dominated peoples of Europe."

"Well, if you want me to do a job," Steve said slowly, "you know I'll do my best. What is it?"

"I want you to be one of the fliers who ferry bombers to England." Major Sears looked up quickly as the Navy man spoke. "You can see what valuable experience you'll get."

"Ferry bombers to England?" Steve gasped. His eyes shone and he turned to Sears. "Will you give me a crack at it, Major?"

"After reading this report, I'd be tempted to give

you a crack at anything you asked for." Watching the lanky young American narrowly, Major Sears warned him somberly, "Remember, it's dangerous work. And for you it may prove to be heartbreaking work."

"Steve can take it," Commander Bennett broke in quickly. "He can take it as well as dish it out."

"I'm ready to take my chance along with the rest," Steve said.

"Well—" Major Sears hesitated and his expression had a curious sadness in it. He turned to Bennett. "Isn't the boy too young for such a——"

"That's a mark in favor of both him and the idea," Commander Bennett put in quickly. He explained to Steve, "Major Sears and I grew up together. When the last war broke out, he being a British subject entered the Royal Naval Air Service. I went to Annapolis. We've kept in close touch with each other, and recently, when he was down in Washington, Major Sears told me about a problem that faces him."

"We've been losing bombers," Sears said gravely, "under mysterious conditions."

"What do you mean?" Steve asked.

"I'm not sure. Until three months ago we had a perfect record. Then we lost one bomber. Two weeks later we lost two more. The number has been rising steadily ever since." Sears tapped the desk with two brown fingers. "We know positively the losses are not due to mechanical difficulties."

"Then what are they due to?" Steve demanded.

"That's what I believe you may be able to discover," Commander Bennett declared. "Are you game to try?"

"I am."

"Are you ready to leave for Newfoundland at once?"

"Yes."

"Look here, Steve," Major Sears said, "I want you to think this whole thing over very carefully. Let's put it this way. You will come up to our base in Newfoundland with me. If, up to the very second you're to hop off for England, you decide you don't want the job, tell me. I will understand and I won't blame you. And remember," he amended, turning to Commander Bennett, "you must agree that his decision not to make the flight will in no way influence you if he applies for admission to the United States Navy Air Corps."

"Agreed."

"That's very considerate of you, sir," Steve said, "but I've made my decision and I won't change it."

"I told you he could take it," Bennett told Sears. "That, plus his ability to land on his feet, makes him your man."

"Suppose you pick up your things then and meet

me at the airport in an hour," Sears suggested. "We'll take the three o'clock plane for Montreal."

"Fine." Steve rose and held out his hand to Commander Bennett. "Thanks for giving me this chance, sir. And as soon as the job is done, I'm going to hound you for an appointment to Pensacola."

"You won't have to hound me," Commander Bennett promised.

As Steve left the room, Major Sears leaned over Commander Bennett's desk. "Norman, your plan is perfect so far as I can see—except for one thing. If it blasts that boy's career or costs him his life, I shall feel guilty for the rest of *my* life."

"You yourself said that this was war, not a tea party," the Navy man reminded him. "Besides, the whole thing was my idea. I thought of the plan and I provided the man most likely to succeed with it. I'll take full responsibility."

"Just the same, I hate the part I'm going to have to take in it," Sears said as he shook hands grimly with his friend. "You introduced me as Major Sears. If anything goes wrong, if any one of a thousand things go wrong, you should have introduced me as Major Death!"

II.

Steve Meets His Crew

DOWN through the Newfoundland mists twisted the five-place monoplane. It found a break in the heavy clouds and dropped to about 500 feet. Circling the field, the pilot set the plane down and taxied across the field to a low rambling building.

Unseen by Steve Knight, Bofors guns had covered them from concealed anti-aircraft pits until their identity was completely established. As the plane slowed, a ground crew ran out to take the plane in hand and an infantry detail with rifles inconspicuously ready watched Steve and two other pilots climb out. The infantry men came to attention as Major Sears dropped to the ground.

At Sears' signal, an orderly stepped forward. The major said crisply, "Gentlemen, you will be shown to your quarters. I have a report to make out, but will see you this evening. All three of you are in Captain McDonald's flight."

"Will you follow me, please," the orderly said and led the way.

Lugging his grip, Steve and his two companions fell into step behind the orderly. They were led to a ramshackle two-story building.   Halting outside a door on the upper floor, the orderly consulted his list.   He raised his eyes to the ceiling and sang out:

"Mr. Knight's room, sir."

"I'm Knight.   Thanks."

Saluting, the orderly wheeled and led the other two pilots to the next room where he repeated the process.   Steve entered his room.   It was the sort of thing you might expect to find in an inexpensive seashore hotel.   A single iron bed, one chair, a bureau and washstand combined made up the room's furnishings.   A gas mask in a shiny metal case hung from a nail and looked strangely out of place.

Steve dropped his bag and pulled off his coat.   He had just shoved his hat on the back of his blond head and was staring around the room a second time when there was a knock at the door.

"Come in."

A tall thin man entered.   He smiled at Steve and asked, "Are you Steve Knight?"

"Yes."

"That's luck.   I'm Hugh Gracey.   I'm to be your first officer."

"My what?" Steve asked as he put out his hand to meet Gracey's.

"First officer.   Each pilot has a first officer, or co-pilot, and a radio operator.   Merlin, your radioman, should be along any minute."

"How did you know about me?"

"I fancy Major Sears radioed ahead. McDonald has already made up the assignments for you three chaps who just arrived. Very enterprising fellow, McDonald. You'll like him."

"I guess I will from what the Major told me on the trip down from Montreal," Steve agreed. "Say, have you ever made the hop?"

"Yes, but only twice."

"Only!"

"Some of the men around here have made eight or nine hops, and five is more or less the average," Hugh Gracey explained. There was a knock. "That would be Corky Merlin."

As Steve called, "Come in!" the door opened and a little monkey of a man entered. He screwed up his eyes and gave Steve a quick penetrating glance. Then he smiled.

" 'Ullo. You're Knight, I suppose," he remarked with more than a trace of cockney accent. He held out his hand. "Pleased to meet you."

"Knight, this is Corky Merlin," said Gracey. "The most unmitigated liar and the best radioman under any hat and over any shoes."

" 'Ere, 'ere! None of that now. I won't 'ave me reputation blarsted like that." He turned and regarded Steve shrewdly. "You're a bit young, but I think you'll do," he remarked bluntly.

"Perhaps I should have added that Corky is noted for his frankness," Hugh Gracey amended.

"Per'aps you should 'ave added that we're going over tonight," Corky Merlin corrected. He sat himself primly on the edge of Steve's bed, asking, "Well, young 'un, what do you say to that?"

"Swell. But what are we flying?"

"Consolidated B–24's," Gracey declared.

"That's great. I'm glad I'm getting a ship I know. Now," Steve looked from one to the other, "what can you tell me that I ought to know?"

"Not much," Gracey said. "We'll wander over to McDonald's office in a moment or two. The flying orders are remarkably simple. Corky handles the radio end, I handle the navigation, and you handle the stick for about six of the eight hours it takes us."

"Everything's simply ducky," Merlin scoffed, "provided the Jerries don't get us."

"What Corky means," Gracey explained, "is that we carry no arms of any sort. If we're attacked, we must just cut and run for it."

"You mean we don't carry any machine guns?" Steve asked incredulously. Both Corky and Hugh Gracey nodded silently. "That's tough. I took a special course in gunnery, aerial gunnery, and developed into a fair marksman. I got shot down once when I was unarmed and I wouldn't want it to happen again."

"That's perfectly understandable," Gracey commented dryly. "Where were you shot down?"

"Over the Honduras jungle. I'll tell you about it some time."

"Blimey," Corky moaned. " 'E's another of them conversation pilots."

"Oh, ease off," Gracey ordered the radioman. "Let's trot over and talk to McDonald."

"That's worse than flak when you've made a fool of yourself," Corky said.

"What's flak?" Steve asked.

"Anti-aircraft fire," Gracey explained. "One thing about it, we won't run into flak on this detail and we're not likely to see any Schmitts either."

"Schmitts," Steve guessed, "are Messerschmitts?"

"Right." Gracey led them to a small frame office. Just before he opened the door, he said, "Don't let Corky's wild talk worry you. McDonald's an excellent commander and a stout chap."

"Just don't make a fool of yourself," Corky warned. "He'll take the hide off you."

"As you should know," Gracey reminded him, opening the door. "He's done it to you."

They stepped into a small, bare office. Three men huddled over a map that was spread out across a crude pine table. One of them was Major Jeff Sears and he straightened up when he recognized Steve.

"Just the men we were looking for," Sears said.

"Glad to see you three got together. Mac, this is Steve Knight."

"How do you do," McDonald greeted Steve gravely. He was a spare man of medium height with steady gray eyes. He looked at Steve, and then smiled abruptly. "Glad you're with us."

"Thank you, sir."

"As you may have heard," Sears remarked, "you three are to hop off tonight."

"I have heard," Hugh Gracey replied. "We're quite prepared."

"Good," McDonald said brusquely. "Knight, I believe you can safely trust the navigating to Gracey. And they say Merlin is a good radioman, though personally, I doubt it. But as for the actual flying—that's on your shoulders."

"Yes, sir."

"We all hop off together," McDonald continued, "but I may as well warn you now, we inevitably become separated. However, just before we leave, you will be given a Very signal pistol and a schedule of the signals which change every hour. Try to keep with me, but don't worry too much if you can't."

"Yes, sir."

"Any questions?"

Gracey kicked Steve's foot and the young American got the signal. He said, "No, sir."

"Right. Then I shall expect you at the starting line in twenty minutes," McDonald said.

Twenty minutes!   Steve, Hugh Gracey and Corky went back to their quarters at a dogtrot.   Twenty minutes!   Why Steve hadn't even unpacked his bag.

"What should I take with me?" Steve asked.

"Nothing but your tooth brush," Gracey said. "I'll meet you at the foot of the stairs and help you pick out a flying outfit."

"Check."   They went into the ramshackle building and Steve started upstairs.   "See you in a couple of minutes."

Entering his room on the second floor, Steve yanked open his bag.   His hands shook with excitement as he pawed through, looking for his tooth brush.

In twenty minutes—no, in eighteen minutes, he'd be shoving off.   Twenty-two years before, from almost this same spot, Alcock and Brown had taken off for their epoch-making flight that ended in an Irish peat bog.   And here he was, Steve Knight, following the trail they blazed.

"But not to a peat bog, I hope," he muttered.

Flying had changed plenty since then.   No longer was it sufficient to have plenty of nerve and be able to handle a ship.   No longer were successful fliers glorified stunt men.   Now it required training and knowledge, and a well-grounded understanding of aerodynamics.

"Hey, Steve Knight," someone shouted from below.

Steve looked quickly around the room. It might be the last time he ever saw it—whoa! That was kid stuff. He dashed out into the hall and down the stairs. Gracey was waiting for him.

"In the early days of this ferry bomber business," Gracey observed, "they didn't have time to provide the boys with suits. From what I hear, a fine collection of outfits went over on the first hop."

"My stuff is upstairs in my bag," Steve said.

"Use our stuff, it will save wear and tear on your own."

They entered a big room and a soldier stepped forward. The inverted wishbones on his sleeve identified him as a sergeant. He saluted Gracey smartly.

"Sergeant, can you fit out Mr. Knight?"

"Yes, sir." The sergeant looked Steve over critically. "Right over here, sir."

Flying suits lay piled up on tables. The sergeant led the way unerringly to a table and picked out a suit which he held up to Steve.

"This ought to fit."

Steve slipped into the wool-lined leather suit and closed the zippers. The supply sergeant looked pleased with himself.

"Does it fit all right?" Gracey asked.

"Perfect," replied Steve.

"Then let's go."

"Will you sign for it?" the sergeant asked as they walked down the aisle between the rows of tables covered with suits of all sizes. He held out a big ledger, pointing to the place. "Right there, sir."

Steve signed and they went out.

As Steve and Hugh Gracey walked along, they saw other men in flying outfits headed in the same direction. Steve looked up. The sky was cloudless— perfect for their purpose. In a few minutes he'd be up there. And eight or nine hours from now, he'd be setting down his big four-motored B–24 on England's beleaguered soil.

III.

The Jump-Off

THIRTY-FIVE men gathered around their flight commander for last minute instructions.

"Most of you have made this trip before and know the ropes, but don't get careless. Remember, don't fly over ships or towns. I don't want you knocked down by anti-aircraft fire." McDonald looked from man to man. "Now—each navigator has his sealed orders. Thumbs up! And good luck."

"Thumbs up," the crews chorused.

Scattering to their planes, they prepared for the big hop. McDonald accompanied Steve and Gracey to the big bomber which was to take them over. He walked with his arm over Steve's shoulders.

"Sorry I haven't had more time to talk with you, Steve, but this is a rush job more or less."

"I think we'll make out," Steve assured him.

"I know you will. You've got a good crew and I hear you've handled these big Consolidated ships before."

"Yes, I have."

"Splendid. You're Number Twelve in the jump-off. Good luck."

Steve gave the thumbs-up signal and climbed into the plane. Turning, McDonald sprinted to his own ship.

Steve looked at the gauges and saw that everything was in readiness for the take-off. He smiled as he thought that only a short time before the myriad instruments and controls in the pilot's cockpit of the average bomber, or transport, meant absolutely nothing to him. Now each dial, each control was a friend ready to do its part to make the trip a success.

Thanks to the B–24's tricycle landing gear, he was able to look around the field and really see more of it than he had at any time since his arrival. It was a huge place. New York City's La Guardia Airport could be lost in one corner of Newfoundland's Hatties Field. However, all the buildings had that strange air of impermanence that resulted from hasty construction.

Corky Merlin came from the rear of the plane and leaned over the back of Steve's seat. "Radio all correct, sir," he said—and with a start, Steve realized that he, Steve Knight, was in command. The responsibility of a successful flight rested on his shoulders.

"Thanks, Corky."

"I'm to open the orders as soon as we get upstairs," Hugh Gracey said, taking the copilot's seat. A motor roared. "There goes McDonald."

A plane roared down the runway. It took off

sluggishly and climbed slowly due to the heavy load of fuel it carried.

"What gas are we working on?" Steve asked.

"Octane rating." Gracey replied and Steve nodded. "100 for the take-off and 90 for cruising."

"Swell."

Another plane roared into the sky. Then another and another.

Steve's ground crew looked up at him. He gave the signal and the starters ground. The four motors turned over, caught, and roared. He throttled down and watched the gauges which showed how many revolutions per minute he was getting from each motor. They were turning easily.

"There goes Number Nine," Hugh Gracey pointed out.

Conscious of mounting excitement, Steve searched the faces of his gauges for the hundredth time to be sure that everything was set for the big hop. Another plane took off. Then Number Eleven followed.

"Okay," Steve said. "Hold your hats."

While the ground crew stepped back, Steve opened up with all four motors, turned the single wheel under the nose, and kicked the rudder. The big plane lumbered around and rolled forward to the starting line.

Before him stretched a runway 5,000 feet long and 1,200 feet wide. He was given the signal. The B–24 started down the runway exactly eleven minutes after McDonald had taken to the air.

Guard lights flashed along the runway borders turning from amber to green at every 1,000 feet. Faster and faster they went. Now the vibration from the undercarriage had vanished. That meant they were off the ground.

Holding at about a five-degree climb, Steve rose slowly. He circled Hatties Field once as the eleven other planes had done. And then headed the big Consolidated B–24, which the R.A.F. had rechristened the Liberator, into the gathering dusk.

The twelve-plane flight was winging eastward in a wide echelon formation. "George," the automatic Sperry gyropilot, was doing the flying, and they were hitting along at 10,000 feet altitude.

"How's about some vanilla ice cream?" Steve asked into the mouthpiece as he sighted a heavy bank of cumulus clouds ahead.

Hugh Gracey looked puzzled, and asked, "What's that?"

"Ice cream," Steve repeated, pointing to the cumulus ahead. Gracey's laugh crackled in the earphones.

Ahead of them they could see McDonald's ship dropping to avoid the cloud bank. Now the others had started down. Steve followed suit. Number Eleven plane, about 500 feet to his left, dipped a second later.

The tail wind that was helping push them along was also moving the cumulus just fast enough so that it seemed hours before the flight caught up to it. By this time, McDonald had taken them down to about 2,500 feet. Only a short way below was the stratus. Was McDonald going to take them into that Steve wondered?

"This weather is perfect for our show," Gracey observed. "Daylight up to nine o'clock."

"Is it much tougher when the days are shorter?" Steve asked.

"Much," was Gracey's clipped rejoinder.

"The light's going fast," came Corky Merlin's voice from the radio compartment. "I just took a look at it from the rear gunner's cockpit."

"The light's going and so is McDonald," Steve muttered.

Up ahead, the flight commander's plane was still dropping. In another minute it would be lost to sight in the fleecy stratus cloud bank. That meant more work for Steve and his crew.

"What's he up to?" Gracey asked. "We're well below the cumulus."

"Not low enough, I guess," Steve replied.

"There goes Mac, the bounder," Corky announced as McDonald slipped out of sight. "Never trust a blooming Scotsman, especially when 'e's a blinking Australian Scotsman as well."

"He knows what he's doing," Steve commented shortly. "Well, here we go."

Their big Consolidated seemed to rip the woolly stratus to shreds. Down, down, down they went. Steve was anxious to get through and pick up the flight again. It proved to be a thick bank. The top had been at about 2,000 feet—the altimeter showed 800 feet when they came out below it.

And it was dark down here. No planes showed up ahead. All three peered to the left. Five minutes went by, but Number Eleven plane didn't appear. Steve glanced at Gracey.

"Now what?" he asked. "Are we supposed to go topside again and look around for them?"

"No. In case we become separated, we're expected to carry on. We may pick them up later."

"I'm going up just for luck," Steve observed.

"I 'ope you don't run into Number Eleven coming down," Corky said.

Climbing slowly, Steve cut through the cloud bank. He climbed right through it to 3,000 feet without sighting the flight or any individual planes. Grinning at Hugh Gracey, he said:

"Guess we're on our own from here out."

"McDonald's an old woman about cumulus," Gracey sighed disgustedly. "Now I've got to go to work."

"Anything coming over the air?" Steve asked.

"Not for us," Corky replied. "Some blasted baseball scores, but who cares about them?"

"I do," Steve yelped. "Who's leading the American League?"

"What a question to ask a poor benighted heathen like Corky," Gracey chuckled. "He thinks the American League is a unit of distance."

"What rot! I know perfectly well what the Hamerican League is," Corky replied hotly. "It's that meeting of all the Hamerican republics your President Roosevelt held in Cuba a year or so ago."

"What did I tell you?" Gracey asked. "The Pan-American Conference and the American League both mean the same to him."

"I guess what we're doing is more important than my finding out who's leading," Steve said. He glanced at his watch. "Come on, Hugh. Time to check the instruments and bring the navigation log up to date."

"This is one part of the trip I abhor," Gracey remarked. "This business of checking twenty-six instruments every half-hour is a bore."

"It's better than finding ourselves in Africa because of a change in the wind drift," Steve laughed.

As soon as that chore had been taken care of and Corky had completed the radio log, Steve stretched one arm at a time. He looked pointedly at his watch and glanced at his copilot. Hugh Gracey grinned and slipped into the right-hand seat.

"My trick, eh?"

"Yep. Have you worked out the navigation data?"

"I have it right here."

"Good. Take over for a half-hour, will you?"

After the next instrument check, Steve returned to the controls. They flew on and on with nothing around them but emptiness. Every half-hour they went through the navigation and instrument ritual.

Around midnight, they took turns at the tomato soup, coffee, and chocolate bars that had been packed for them. And each had about an hour's rest on a cot between ten o'clock and four the next morning.

But when it came Steve's turn to lie down, he found he couldn't sleep. The trip was uneventful, almost monotonous, not at all as he had expected. Here he was—flying the Atlantic! Yet he had no particular sense of excitement or adventure.

Just the same, he found it impossible to sleep. Maybe there was more kick to this business than he realized; or perhaps the sense of his responsibility made sleep out of the question. He was glad when he could return to the controls.

Hugh Gracey handed him the last minute data on their flight. They were forced to hold the ship a bit to the south to avoid being drifted off their course by the wind. Steve settled down to the job. In a few more hours, they'd be there.

IV.

Welcome Committee—with Fire

IT WAS growing light again. Not light enough really to see very much, but light enough to tell Steve that dawn had broken and soon would illumine the whole sky.

Both Hugh Gracey and Corky were on the alert and strangely tense. They stared out of the side windows and watched the air around them. Steve noticed that, for the most part, they peered upward.

"What's the matter? Do you expect to see England up there?"

"Look here, old boy, you may not realize it, but the Jerries have a nasty habit of sending out heavy bombers to raid shipping west of Ireland," Gracey explained. "If it's all the same to you, I'd rather not bump into one of them. Nasty beggars."

"Say, I'd forgotten all about that. This trip has been such a push-over I was beginning to think it was highly overrated. Is there really a chance we might bump into one of your 'nasty beggars'?"

"An excellent chance. You're not being paid your salary just to ferry a plane across the Atlantic. Some of that money is to repay you for the risk you take from attack."

"The Jerries don't like these Liberators," Corky declared. "Hi 'aven't a doubt but that they'd give a bucketful of their blarsted Hiron Crosses to the bloke that brought one down."

"Well, you fellows may be right about the risk we're running, but so far this trip has been tamer than flying figure eights over a corn patch." Steve nodded to the growing light. "One thing about it, in another ten or fifteen minutes, we'll be able to see any attacker a mile——"

"Here he comes," Hugh Gracey cut in, his low voice tense. "Above us—on the right—300 feet or more."

Instinctively, Steve put the ship into a steep turn to the left. He cut out of it with a wing-over and looked up. A yellow projectile flashed past them.

Evidently their attacker had felt so confident that he was unobserved, the quick maneuver had taken him completely by surprise. Steve gave his ship the gun and streaked eastward, full-out. Hugh Gracey ran to the rear gunner's cockpit.

"Can we run away from him?" Steve asked.

"'Fraid not, old man," came Gracey's calm voice through the headphone. "Strange thing. Our chap is a single-place seaplane."

"That means he can't carry much fuel."

"Right."

"Think we can keep far enough away from him to exhaust his fuel?" Steve asked.

"Well," Gracey said slowly, "it's worth trying, don't you think?"

"And how," Steve breathed fervently.

His four motors were turning over beautifully, but were they turning over fast enough? Could they turn over fast enough to prevent a speedy little single-place fighter from overtaking them?

Speed was their only protection. Not again would the enemy pilot be caught flat-footed by anything Steve could do. And he could never hope to outstunt the yellow fighter with his big bomber. If that baby could get on his tail—but he hadn't done so yet, Steve reminded himself.

"Where is he now?" he asked Gracey.

"Overhauling us."

"Hi'd give my blarsted right arm for a machine gun," Corky groaned. "Just one, that's hall Hi arsk."

"Keep your arm," Gracey advised him. "You'll need it to swim with—if you get a chance to swim."

"Where is he now?" Steve asked. "How far behind us?"

"I'd judge we have a lead of about 1,500 to 2,000 feet."

"Just one gun," Corky was praying. "Give me just one gun, one gun."

Steve glanced at the altimeter—12,000 feet. Could he escape by diving through the clouds below?

"Now where is he?"

"Right on our tail. Not 1,000 feet away."

"Get out of there, Hugh. He'll get you when he opens fire."

"Here he comes," Gracey cried.

Steve did a snap roll and then sideslipped.

"He's firing," Gracey reported in his calm voice. "He's still following."

A wild Immelmann failed to shake him. Steve whipped the big ship from side to side trying to get away from the speedy little plane that stuck to them like death itself. He couldn't tell whether they'd been hit yet. If they had, the hits weren't vital— every control responded normally.

"Look out," Gracey warned. "He's closing in for the kill."

Corky railed impotently at their inability to fight back. And Gracey, with never a tremor in his voice, kept Steve posted of their attacker's every move— and how he clung to them despite Steve's desperate stunting.

But one couldn't jack the B–24 all over the sky like a pursuit ship. It was only a question of time. Their attacker feinted and Steve spun the big plane out of the line of fire. But before it had recovered from the maneuver, the little plane darted in and Hugh Gracey announced again:

"Here he comes."

Again Steve managed to avoid the fatal burst that would send them down, out of control—the plane a smoking, flaming ruin that only the Atlantic below could quench. Again the little plane feinted. And again Gracey reported:

"Here he——"

Hugh Gracey didn't finish. Steve felt something give, but he didn't know what. Smoke, then flame, burst from the extreme left motor. And Corky was babbling:

"He got Hugh, the murdering beggar! He got——"

Cutting the ignition, Steve turned the ship on its nose and let it drop through the clouds below.

Gracey had fallen to the floor of the rear cockpit. Now he came sliding along the catwalk. Corky held on for dear life. The plane was at too much of an angle for him to be able to fight his way to where Gracey lay wedged, bleeding badly.

They knifed through the clouds. But Steve let the plane drop. He eased back on the stick very slightly. A moment later the little yellow plane popped through the clouds after them. And still they fell. Still smoke poured from the left motor.

Watching the plane above, Steve saw him turn and head westward. That was what he wanted.

They were a scant hundred feet from the lashing waves below them, waves that seemed to reach up for them with angry, white-topped fingers, when Steve pulled out of the dive. He cut in the three remaining motors, snapped over his shoulder to Corky:

"Get Hugh."

"Yes, sir."

Far ahead, the yellow plane was winging westward. That was strange. But Steve had no time now to worry about such a seeming contradiction or wonder what it meant. Corky carried Gracey down and laid him gently on the deck behind Steve.

"Is he badly hurt?"

"Very bad."

"Think he'll live?"

There was a second's silence before Corky croaked, "Hi don't know. 'E's bad 'urt."

"Want to try and make England or stick with the murdering bum that got us?"

"What do you mean?"

"I mean go after the Jerry that blew us down. He can't fly around forever. Another brush with us and he'll be out of gas."

"And when 'e is?" Corky asked quietly.

"Then it will be our turn to get tough."

"Right-ho man, Steve. Let's get tough."

Skimming along barely 50 feet above the white caps, Steve blessed the fact that the B–24 was painted a mottled grayish blue. And that gave him an idea. Naval planes were usually painted orange or yellow so that in case they were forced down, they would show up against the sea. Their attacker was yellow from nose to tail. Yet it was impossible that he was operating from an airplane carrier. And they should be still too far from shore for his limited fuel capacity.

The left engine had stopped smoking. That was a help. And their one-plane reception committee was winging along ahead evidently secure in the belief that he had shot down another bomber. He had seemed in a hurry to fly away—another indication that he might be nearing the end of his fuel.

One thing was certain—he'd never spot the B–24 if he looked back.

Corky was working over Hugh Gracey with a first-aid kit. Steve heard him puffing and cursing as he fought to stop the flow of blood from Gracey's wounds.

His plan—if you could call it a plan—was wild and impossible. All Steve knew or cared was that for the second time in his flying career he had been attacked when he was unarmed.

He was filled with a blind, unreasoning determination to strike back. That he would surely wreck the bomber didn't matter. That he and Corky, as well as Hugh Gracey, would pay the penalty never entered his mind.

Far ahead the yellow plane was seen to falter. It was slanting down. And then Steve could see that its propeller was slowing down, was stopping. He was out of fuel. This was their chance.

Steve was watching the yellow plane so intently

that he failed to see a vessel lying low in the water ahead. The yellow plane drifted down while the B–24 with three of its motors functioning was fast overhauling it. Corky's shout broke the spell.

"Look! A boat!"

Steve's concentration on the yellow plane was broken. He glanced down and saw what appeared to be a large fishing boat dead ahead. So that explained the yellow plane and its pontoons. Now he noticed an oil slick around the ship. The yellow plane was headed for it.

There was sudden activity on the vessel. That meant they had sighted the B–24. But even now the yellow fighter was unaware that he had been followed. Steve climbed slightly.

The yellow seaplane settled down and bounced on the oily slick. Steve had only gained 200 feet, but that was plenty for his purpose. A gun was being cleared on the foreward deck of the vessel.

"You're too late, my friend," Steve exulted. "You're too late."

"Crash them, Stevie my boy," Corky urged. "Crash the whole bleeding lot of them."

"There's my meat," Steve cried as he pointed the nose of the big bomber at the tiny yellow seaplane bouncing on the swells below. He opened the throttle.

There was one burst of fire from the ship. Then it stopped. Steve was roaring down at the fighter and to fire meant certain death to their own man. Steve yelled:

"Hang on to Hugh!"

The yellow plane was getting bigger and bigger. This would fix him. No more shooting down un-armed planes for either the pilot or his ship. Steve's plane was diving full-out. He held the nose steady on the yellow seaplane.

"Crash 'im, crash 'im. Crash the blarsted mur-derer," Corky was chanting. He held Hugh Gracey cradled in his arms, held him so that when they struck the yellow monoplane it was he who would take the shock and not the wounded copilot. "Crash 'im, boy, crash 'im."

Suddenly the pilot of the yellow plane became aware of his danger. Steve could see him fighting desperately to free himself of his safety belt, then fighting to get the plastic slide panel open and dive into the sea before death and destruction in the form of the plunging B—24 was upon him.

"You'll never make it," Steve gloated savagely. The yellow plane was a scant 200 feet away. "I've got you, I've got you."

And then it happened.

Just as victory was within his grasp, just when it seemed that no power could save the seaplane or its pilot, Steve felt the big bomber lurch. It swung off its yellow target.

Steve fought the controls, got back on the target

again. Something had given way, the bomber seemed almost alive and was struggling to veer and sideslip to the right. Steve glanced out—the left motor was gone!

It was the loss of the motor that had unbalanced the ship. It veered away from the yellow plane. Once more Steve dragged it back. And suddenly the bomber spun around as though flipped by huge invisible fingers.

There was a splintering, rending crash. A sheet of water shot skyward. For a moment the plane disappeared below the surface only some fifty feet from its target. Down came the water splashed up by its dive to hide the bomber momentarily as it rose sluggishly to the surface.

A wave washed over them as they floated low in the water. Green water smashed at the windows and tore at the wings. The controls, their wires snapped, whipped about as the wave battered the rudder, elevator and ailerons.

As the wave passed, Steve looked at Corky. The little cockney's face was chalk-white and dejected. He caught the glint of hot tears in the young American's eyes.

"You couldn't 'elp it," he declared stoutly. "Just our blooming luck, that's hall."

"You know what this means, don't you?" Steve snapped.

Nodding glumly, Corky looked toward the vessel.

Already a boat was being lowered away and armed sailors were jumping into it. Steve followed his gaze and choked. What rotten luck! What incredibly rotten luck.

Suddenly he ripped at his safety belt, tore it loose. He dove into the bombardier's cockpit in the plane's nose. He kicked futilely at the plastic panels, but their strength and the pressure of the water made it impossible to break them. He dashed back to the pilot's cockpit and heaved at the lever that opened the bomb door. The water held the bomb racks tightly closed.

Looking out, Steve saw that the sailors had floated their boat and were pulling toward them. Sweat streaked his grimy face as he tugged at the lever, muttering:

"They're not going to get this plane. They're not going to have a chance to examine my ship."

" 'Urry," Corky urged, " 'urry!"

The door to the bomb rack opened almost unwillingly. Water began to pour into the plane's belly. Steve opened the cabin door and signaled the boat. He felt better now.

"Anyway," he told Corky over his shoulder, "we'll be able to get Hugh attended to."

"That's a blessing," Corky replied. He sighed. "Hi never thought Hi'd end up a blinking prisoner of war."

V.

Mystery Ship

AS THE boat pulled closer, Steve saw that all the sailors were in civilian clothes. The man standing in the bow held a very uncivilian submachine gun pointed at them, but his rough sweater and dungarees suggested that he was a peaceful fisherman.

In English, though with a heavy accent, he called out, "Ahoy, bomber. You surrender—yes?"

"What else can we do?" Steve called back bitterly. "Come on, we're unarmed and we've got a wounded man here."

Despite his assurance, the sailor continued to cover him with the submachine gun and the oarsmen rowed slowly and cautiously. The helmsman, who seemed in charge, rapped out his commands in German as the lifeboat drew alongside.

"Pass out the wounded man first," the helmsman ordered in good English.

One of the sailors held the boat to the plane by clinging to the open door. The boat bobbed up and down beside the waterlogged plane, and passing Hugh Gracey to the outstretched hands of two sailors was a ticklish operation. Gracey's eyes fluttered open once and he clamped his teeth on a groan.

Corky followed Gracey into the lifeboat. Steve took one last look around at the slowly sinking plane and jumped after him. A sailor put his oar against the plane and shoved off. Sitting between two oarsmen on the row back to the fishing vessel, Steve stared at the bomber. It had been such a beautiful ship; it had handled like a dream; and there it went, to the bottom, when its destination had been England.

Steve looked up and found the helmsman watching him with an unpleasantly triumphant expression. The man was gloating, gloating over the bomber's fate and over the fact that Steve, Hugh and Corky were prisoners. It was hard to take and Steve looked away.

The lifeboat bumped against the side of the fishing vessel. A tall straight man with iron-gray hair leaned over the rail and gave orders as Hugh Gracey was raised gently to the deck. Corky and Steve followed. The gray-haired man gave an order in German. The helmsman saluted and the boat turned to pick up the pilot of the yellow seaplane and tow it to the vessel.

"Take him below and have his wounds attended to," the gray-haired man ordered in English. He bowed stiffly to Steve and Corky, announced, "I am Captain Hansler. Who are you?"

"I'm Steve Knight. I was the pilot. The wounded man is Hugh Gracey, my first officer and navigator. This is Corky Merlin, my radio operator."

"Gentlemen." Captain Hansler saluted them. "You are, of course, prisoners of war. You will remain with us until we are relieved by another vessel, when you will be taken to the Reich. How soon we shall be relieved, I cannot tell."

"I guess it doesn't matter much," Steve said dejectedly.

"I sympathize with you," Hansler said. It sounded sincere. "In the last war, I was held prisoner by the British for sixteen months. I will try to see that you receive as fair treatment now as I received then."

"Thank you, sir."

"I regret that limitations of space may work a hardship on you, but such are the fortunes of war." Captain Hansler summoned a sailor. "Take these gentlemen to the first officer's quarter."

Clicking his heels, the sailor turned stiffly and led Steve and Corky down a companionway. He held open the door to a small cabin and motioned them to step inside. The door closed behind them and they heard the key click into place and the grate of the lock.

"Guess they want us to stay here," Steve observed dryly.

He sat down on the edge of a double-decker bunk and looked around the small cabin. The cabin, he decided, wasn't more than ten feet long by five feet wide. In addition to the two bunks, one above the other, it had a high narrow closet that formed the foot of the bunks, a desk that folded against the wall, a camp stool, and a porthole.

Going to the porthole, he looked out. The lifeboat was towing the yellow seaplane up to the ship. Steve beckoned to Corky to join him and signaled for silence. Before going to the porthole, Corky hung his helmet on the doorknob so that it covered the keyhole.

Once the plane was beside the ship, it was almost impossible to see what was going on. However, Steve did see a sailor fasten a loop of cable to the tip of one wing. A moment later someone sang out an order and they heard the pound of a donkey engine and the creak of a derrick. The yellow plane rose from the water. A second later it was swung out of sight.

"So that's how it's done," Steve breathed. "This innocent-looking fishing ship, or whatever it is, has a derrick. I wonder if it has a catapult."

"Hi didn't see one," Corky whispered. "But blimey, Hi didn't see the derrick when we come aboard neither."

"That's just the point," Steve declared, "they keep it out of sight somehow. To all appearances this is a peaceful ship engaged in fishing. I'll bet the ship's ownership papers would make interesting reading."

" 'ow do you mean?"

"Why, this boat is probably registered in the name of some dummy owner and flies a neutral flag. Yes, and in a pinch, I'll bet they could scare up a few barrels of fish to make their presence out here look on the level."

"Hi wonder 'ow many of our chaps they've shot down?"

"Plenty. They catch you early in the morning just when the trip is beginning to slow down your alertness and reactions and—bang! They didn't have much trouble with us, did they?"

"They would 'ave if we'd 'ad some guns," Corky assured him.

"But we didn't and they knew it."

Going back to the bunk, Steve slouched down on it dejectedly, then climbed slowly out of his hot flying suit. Corky prowled around the cabin examining everything.

"Wonder what's 'appened to Gracey?" Corky mused. " 'E was in a bad way, poor lad."

"I hope they've got a doctor aboard." Steve laughed without humor as he added, "They probably have. This gang never does things by halves."

Footsteps sounded in the corridor outside and Corky barely had time to snatch his helmet from the doorknob when the key turned in the lock and the door swung open. The helmsman and a man in a worn flying suit entered. As a deterrent in the event that Steve or Corky got ideas about the possibility of escape, the helmsman carried an automatic loosely in his hand.

"You are the pilot?" the helmsman asked Steve.

"Yeah," Steve replied carelessly, lolling back on the bunk.

The man in the flying suit was evidently the pilot of the yellow plane. He said something angrily in German to the helmsman who in turn barked at Steve:

"Stand up in the presence of your betters."

"What betters?" Steve drawled without moving.

The helmsman's face flushed. He backed out of the cabin pushing the pilot ahead of him. As Steve and Corky exchanged puzzled glances, the reason for his retreat was explained. They heard him bark an order and the next moment three burly sailors entered the cabin.

There was barely room for the sailors to move. Two of them went to the bunk and without warning yanked Steve bodily to his feet. They held him upright and the helmsman poked his head in at the door.

"Ah! That is better."

The pilot glanced inside and grinned contentedly. It was useless for Steve to struggle, the two men holding him were too powerful. Besides, he had learned from his adventures in Honduras that an ounce of thinking was worth ten pounds of strength.

The pilot said something to the helmsman who translated in English. "How did you sink your plane and why did you do so?"

"I sank it by opening the bomb trap and I did it just so you'd never have a chance to look it over."

"You have an irritating manner," the helmsman told Steve, "and I am tempted to have my men teach you manners."

"Wait till you get to know me," Corky cut in. "Hi'm twice as irritating a bloke as little Steve 'ere."

Both the helmsman and the pilot regarded the little Englishman coldly a moment. Then, in response to a question from the pilot, the helmsman asked Steve:

"That was a Consolidated B–24 bomber you were flying?"

"Uh—I don't remember," Steve said slowly.

"It is useless to lie. We recognized it."

"Then you know how much trouble those planes have caused you."

"Most irritating," the helmsman remarked to no one in particular. "What are the latest developments on that special plane?"

"Er—I can't recall," Steve drawled.

"You might as well tell me, we know anyway."

"Then why ask me?"

His face suddenly white, the helmsman rapped out

an order. Steve's guards twisted his arms behind his back. The helmsman asked: "Now do you recall any of the B–24's developments?"

"Not a single one."

At a nod one of the guards began to twist his arm. Steve winced but grinned. He grinned straight at the helmsman.

"Now do you recall its developments?"

"I've got a lousy memory." The twisting was pretty bad, but Steve still managed to grin. "Nothing ever—seems to help me—remember."

"You'll remember," the helmsman warned, "or I'll have your arm torn off."

The guard increased the pressure on Steve's arm. Steve found it impossible to grin now and he stared hard at the floor so that his captors couldn't see his eyes water. Slowly the other guard began to twist his left arm.

"Think hard," the helmsman ordered. "Tell us about the plane."

Steve clamped his teeth shut and tried not to let his face betray his pain.

"Think hard. What developments——"

"What is going on here?" Captain Hansler's voice barked.

Immediately the pressure was released on his arms and Steve was unable to stifle his sigh of relief. The captain stepped into the doorway of the cabin and took in the situation at a glance. He turned to the helmsman.

"Lieutenant, you will remember that these men are prisoners of war. How they are treated when we return to port is not our concern, but as long as they are on this vessel, they must be treated with courtesy. Go on deck."

The lieutenant obeyed without a flicker of hesitation. The captain said something to the sailors in German and they squeezed past Corky and left the cabin. Hansler addressed the pilot also in German. Whatever the pilot replied, Captain Hansler nodded briefly and continued down the corridor.

For a moment, the pilot glared at Corky and Steve in turn. Then his glance sharpened as he noticed Steve's new flying suit lying on the bunk. He ran his gaze appraisingly over Steve's lanky body, they were about the same size.

Picking up Steve's suit, the pilot spit on the floor between them and stalked contemptuously from the room.

The door closed and the lock clicked.

Steve dropped down on the edge of the bunk and let his twisted arms hang relaxed at his sides. Draping his helmet over the keyhole again, Corky jumped to his side.

"Hi knew you'd do, young 'un," he whispered. You gave them what for and no mistake."

"They gave me something too," Steve admitted.

" 'Ere, let me rub your arms," Corky suggested.

At the first touch of Corky's strong hands on his wrenched muscles Steve winced, but after a moment the pain disappeared as the little cockney kneaded his arms. Steve relaxed under Corky's ministrations until he felt positively drowsy. He roused himself by asking:

"Say, where did you learn to massage?"

"Hi was a boxing manager and second, 'ad a stable of fighters of my own for a time."

"It's a good trick," Steve murmured. "I feel like a new man."

"Hi'm not through yet. Hi've got to get all the kinks out or you won't be hable to close your blooming 'ands tomorrow. They gave you the works, as you Hamericans say."

"That captain came at just the right moment. You know, he seems like a regular guy."

"Probably one of the old-timers," Corky hazarded, "an Imperial German Navy man with none of this Nazi nonsense to 'im."

"I guess there is a difference," Steve mused.

"Of course there is. Those old-timers were 'ard fighters, but they fought like gentlemen. Nowadays, the young 'uns are being taught to fight like muckers. And this pursecution and hall." Corky shook his head glumly.

"I guess that persecution goes against the grain of every American who knows his history," Steve declared hotly. "Why our country was founded to give people in Europe a place where they could escape that very thing."

"That reminds me." Corky stopped kneading Steve's arms and regarded the young pilot quizzically. "Did you 'appen to catch what Captain Hansler said?"

"What do you mean?"

"Why when 'e ordered that young 'un to treat us like prisoners of war, he added something habout 'ow they are treated when we return to port is not our concern,' " Corky said significantly. "Did you 'ear 'im?"

"I guess I was too busy feeling sorry for myself," Steve admitted. He repeated soberly, " 'How they are treated when we return to port is not our concern.' Hmmm. Corky, that doesn't sound so good."

"It don't and that's a fact."

"All right," Steve said decisively, "that's our cue."

"For what?" Corky asked, eyeing Steve narrowly.

"For escaping."

"Escaping from a blarsted boat. You're daft."

"Maybe, but we've got to try. Now let's see—the first thing we've got to do is——"

The lock clicked. Steve lay back quickly on the bed. Corky got busy searching his clothes for a cigarette. The door opened and a seaman entered carrying a tray.

"Here—iss—your—food," the sailor said concentrating on each word. He unfolded the desk from the wall and put the tray on it. He looked at them and formed words with his lips experimentally before he said, "you—will be—fed—later—again."

"Swell," Steve replied.

"Hi say, me lad, 'ave you got a spare smoke habout you?"

The sailor stared uncomprehendingly at Corky and shrugged his thick shoulders.

"A smoke, fag, cigarette?" Corky made gestures to show a man smoking and the seaman's eyes lighted.

He took four matches from his pocket and held them out to the radioman. Corky held his hand a moment and turned it over. He bowed to the seaman.

"Thank you, pally."

"Thank you, pally," the sailor repeated with a grin. Steve could almost see him tuck away this bit of English in his mind. The sailor went out and locked the door behind him.

"Well," Corky observed, "we've got four matches."

"Yes, but you have no cigarettes to use them on."

"Ho, yes, Hi 'ave. Besides, 'e didn't smoke, there was no stain on 'is fingers." Corky looked at the matches lovingly. "Hi don't quite know 'ow we're going to use these, but they'll come in 'andy."

"Corky, the first thing we must do is find some way to get in touch with Hugh."

"No, sir. The first thing we must do is eat the grub that chap brought us."

That made sense. It was the sort of practical suggestion Venga Savricas might have made, Steve told himself, thinking of his adventures in Honduras with Pedro Hennessey and Savricas, the amazing gypsy. He joined Corky at the desk.

Their food consisted of fish, bread, and two cups of what was supposed to be coffee. The fish and bread were all right, but the ersatz coffee had a faintly acrid flavor as though a generous measure of varnish had been added.

But it was food and they attacked it gratefully. When they finished, Corky leaned back and suddenly there was a cigarette in his hand. Steve laughed and choked on his coffee, and the cockney looked at him suspiciously.

"What's got into you?"

"For a second, you reminded me of a gypsy I met in Central America," Steve explained. "I didn't see you take the cigarette from your pocket and it made me think of Savricas. He did a trick with a cigarette and a match."

"Hi'm not a blinking magician," Corky declared irritably, "but Hi can do a couple of tricks your gypsy feller never 'eard of."

"Such as," Steve baited him.

"Oh-ho! So you think Hi'm bluffing, eh? 'Arf a mo and Hi'll open your eyes."

Fishing around in his pocket, Corky found what he was looking for and held it concealed in his hand. He went to the door and pressed his ear against it. After a moment's listening, he was satisfied that no one was outside.

Leaning back against the door with both hands behind him, Corky studied Steve sleepily. The young pilot's eyes met Corky's and remained fixed on them.

"So your gypsy friend was a wizard, eh?" Corky observed. "Did you 'happen to catch my last name?"

"Sure. Merlin, Corky Merlin."

"Right-ho. Now my hignorant young cub, do you 'appen to know who Merlin was? The horiginal Merlin, the Great Merlin?"

"Why—let's see." Steve puzzled a moment and shook his head. "No, I don't. The name sounds familiar, but I can't place it."

"Merlin," Corky recited, "was the horiginal English wizard. 'E was one of King Harthur's men, a regular miracle worker as ever was. Why, there was nothing that bloke couldn't do. Give 'im a plate and e'd make food appear. Clenched fists opened at 'is glance and locked doors opened at 'is touch— like this."

Stepping suddenly away from the door, Corky turned the knob and swung it open just wide enough for Steve to see that it was unlocked. For a second, he didn't believe his eyes—the door had been locked. And then he could hear Venga Savricas saying, "Always there is explanation." He grinned and Corky closed the door softly.

"Say that's all right. But how did you do it?"

"Magic, young 'un, sheer magic. Hi'm a descendant of Merlin."

"Nuts," Steve scoffed. "Either the guard forgot to lock it or—that's it, you picked the lock."

"True enough."

"Can you pick locks, any lock?"

"Hi wouldn't go so far as to say *hany* lock," Corky said cautiously, "but I can 'andle most of them."

"Then we're in. That does it."

" 'Arf a mo, me lad. Not so fast! We've got a bit more before us than opening doors."

"Sure, but don't forget this—they think we're stuck here in the cabin and can't get out. They're not worrying about us because they think we can't possibly unlock the door. On top of that, they don't see any possible way of our leaving the ship."

"They think we can't leave the ship, eh?"

"Right."

"Well blimey if hi don't think they're right."

Carried away by a feeling of power that Corky could pick locks, Steve had counted on that one fact to set them free. He realized now that he'd gone ahead too fast—there were plenty of hurdles still to be jumped.

"Blimey if hi can see 'ow we'll get off this ship," Corky said. "Do you see a way to do it?"

"We'll do it," Steve assured him. "We'll find some way for the very good reason that we must find a way."

VI.

A Desperate Plan

IT WAS one thing to announce confidently that they'd find a way to escape from their floating prison but it was quite another thing to make good. Steve sat down moodily on the edge of the bunk and tried to figure a way out.

Corky turned to the door and worked on the lock to close it. He made no attempt to shield his movements this time and Steve saw that he had picked the lock with a nail file.

If Corky could open the doors on board, it was up to him to find a way for them to escape, Steve decided. But, as he puzzled over the problem, he became more and more convinced that he had been overly optimistic.

Get off the boat? Why he didn't even know where they were. He had no compass. And land might be a thousand miles in any direction. "Maybe that'll teach you," he told himself, "to keep your mouth shut for a change. I'll get us ashore! And not a pair of water wings between the three of us."

Corky turned from the door and whispered, "Someone's coming." He tiptoed quickly to the porthole and stood looking out. Steve lay back on the bed.

When the door opened, Captain Hansler stood out in the corridor flanked by a pair of seamen. Steve sat up and Corky turned from the porthole to look at him expectantly.

"You may take some exercise on deck now," Captain Hansler said. "But first, would you like to see your friend?"

"Would we?" Steve cried. "You bet we would. How is he?"

"He will recover. However, he lost a lot of blood and is very weak. You may not agree," Hansler smiled wryly, "but it is fortunate that you fell into our hands; otherwise your friend would have—" He snapped his fingers significantly. "Will you follow me?"

Turning, Captain Hansler strode off along the corridor. Steve and Corky fell into single file behind him, and the two husky sailors brought up the rear. Steve did not fail to notice that both were armed. Evidently Hansler was taking no chances.

Halting, Captain Hansler held open a door and bade them enter. He closed the door after them. Hugh Gracey, as white as the sheet pulled up to his chin, lay in a single bed. A man sat beside him. He rose as Steve and Corky entered and bowed stiffly to them.

"I am glad to report that the patient is better," the

man said precisely. "The captain has told you that I was able to remove all the bullets?"

"No," Steve said, "Captain Hansler merely said he was better."

"I see. There were eighteen bullets in his body and four more bullet wounds. Herr Helmuth's aim would seem to be excellent."

"So it would seem," Steve replied. He bent over his sleeping friend. Turning again to the man beside the bed, he held out his hand. "Doctor, I want to thank you for everything you have done."

"I am not a doctor. I was in medical school when war broke out. I am merely a student."

"Just the same," Steve insisted, his hand still extended, "I want to thank you for what you've done."

Ignoring the hand, the student doctor bowed stiffly. "Complications might still set in. Do not thank me until he has fully recovered."

"Have it your way," said Steve, nettled at the man's attitude. Corky was leaning over Hugh Gracey and Steve asked him, "Shall we go now?"

" 'E looks better halreadly. Right-ho, let's go."

"I might point out," the medical student said, "that the captain has turned over his cabin to the patient. I hope our prisoners of war are treated with equal consideration."

"I think they are," Steve assured him sincerely. "I'll thank Captain Hansler for his courtesy."

He matched the medical student's stiff bow and

they went to the door. Captain Hansler and the two sailors were waiting for them in the corridor. Hansler asked:

"How is he now?"

"Pretty weak, I guess, but he was sleeping soundly. Captain, I want to thank you for turning over your cabin to him. I—it was mighty decent of you."

Waving aside Steve's thanks, Hansler murmured, "War's bad enough without being dishonorable enemies. I'm glad your friend will recover."

As they followed the captain up to the deck, Steve asked, "Do I understand that your pilot's name is Helmuth?"

"Yes," Captain Hansler replied shortly.

"He's a very fine flier," Steve remarked and watched for the effect. The captain shrugged.

"Shooting down unarmed planes should not be difficult, should it?"

It was more a statement than a question. "Oh-oh," Steve thought, "so you don't rate Helmuth as a world-beater?" That was an interesting discovery.

Something else Hansler had said stuck in his mind. "Shooting down unarmed planes" were his words. Planes. How many had Helmuth gotten? Flights went over almost nightly. If Helmuth could account for one or two per flight—that might account for the break in the bridge of bombers.

Perhaps this one boat and this one pilot were responsible for all of the bombers which failed to ar-

rive safely in England. Still, it looked like a pretty
expensive way of breaking up the flights of American-
made bombers to Britain.

Reaching the deck, Steve and Corky looked
around curiously. There was no sign of the derrick
which had hoisted Helmuth's yellow seaplane aboard.
And there was no sign of the catapult he must use
to take off. Captain Hansler watched their probing
glances.

"As a flier, you are wondering about the catapult,"
he guessed. "Let me say that I designed this vessel.
It is the most unusual one you have ever seen."

"Hi should say hit is," Corky agreed. He looked
around and asked innocently, "Where did you 'ide
the blooming derrick we 'eard?"

For a moment Captain Hansler was thoughtful.
"I don't believe it will do any harm to tell you that
this ship is in reality two ships."

"Two ships?" Steve asked sharply.

"Yes. From the water line to the top of the main-
mast she's an ordinary fishing vessel," Hansler explained, "But below, she has the draft of a vessel at
least twice her apparent size."

"That explains the amount of room downstairs,"
Steve said.

"Er—by 'downstairs,' I presume you mean below
decks," Hansler replied smiling. "Yes, that explains
it. It explains also how we are able to conceal a seaplane, a derrick, and a catapult."

"Look 'ere now," Corky warned, "you mustn't give away military secrets to the enemy, you know."

"I doubt very much that you'd be able to use any information I might give you. We've been boarded four times and our papers are in perfect order. Besides, the only time we are in any danger is early in the morning when Herr Helmuth is preparing to take off on his—mission."

"Why are you in danger then?" Steve asked.

"Because only then is the catapult in view. A ship must approach us and board us in thirty-two minutes because that's all the time it takes us to conceal the catapult. Once we have done that," Hansler added, "I defy anyone to discover it."

" 'Ow do you work it?" Corky asked.

"Come now, you don't honestly expect me to answer that, do you?"

Evidently, Steve realized, Captain Hansler wasn't giving away as much as he appeared to be. He seemed completely confident that no one could discover the secret of his mystery ship. And if he had been boarded four times without the secret being discovered, he had good cause for his confidence.

A seaman was approaching and Corky asked, "Got a fag you can spare, Captain?"

"Yes." Hansler held out a case and as Corky took one he warned, "Make it last. Cigarettes are a rare luxury."

While Corky lighted it with one of his four precious matches, the seaman saluted Captain Hansler and made some report in German. The captain glanced at Steve who was watching him blankly. Corky was busy with his cigarette.

Turning back to his man, Hansler and he carried on a short conversation. The man saluted and marched off. Hansler turned to his prisoners again.

"Yes, I am very proud of this vessel because I designed it. It is not being used for the purpose I created it for, but—" Hansler shrugged, "my superiors are very pleased with it."

"Do you mean that this one ship and Herr Helmuth have been able to put a dent in the bombers that are being ferried to England?" Steve asked. "Aren't you using any other ships like this one?"

"Surely you do not expect me to answer that question," Hansler said smiling. "Now, if you will excuse me, I shall go below and prepare my reports."

He bowed to them and walked away. The two armed sailors, however, remained at their posts about twenty feet away. Corky wandered to the rail and looked out at the tossing waves.

"They say hit makes you seasick to watch waves," he remarked over his shoulder to Steve, "but Hi don't believe hit."

Steve joined him at the rail and studied the ocean. Out of the corner of his mouth, Corky whispered:

"We're in a fair pickle, Steve, and no mistake. Do you understand German?"

"No, not a word—worse luck."

"Hi understand a bit of the lingo. Do you know what 'Ansler and that other bloke were saying?"

"No. What?"

"From what Hi could gather, this boat is a clearing 'ouse for hinformation habout the bomber flights and convoys. I 'oped something like that was in the offing which is why Hi arsked for a cigarette."

Corky was a man of multiple talents, Steve decided. He hadn't appreciated him before, but now —he could pick locks, speak German. A good solid man to have on your side, Steve thought.

"The bloke that came up to 'Ansler told 'im that the shipping hinformation 'ad come and was 'e to radio it to the subs. Hansler says yes. Then the bloke says as 'ow they still hadn't got final word on the bomber flights leaving 'Atties Field tonight."

"That's interesting. It looks as though this ship had two jobs—to knock down bombers and pass on information." Steve stared out at the waves. "I wish I knew where we were."

"Hi can tell you one thing," Corky said, "we're not moving."

"Not moving? You mean we're anchored here?"

"Hi don't know habout no hanchor, but Hi know we're not moving."

"That still doesn't tell us where—oh-oh," Steve breathed. "Here comes the big shot."

They turned to see Helmuth approaching. The guards straightened up as he reached them and grinned. Evidently Herr Helmuth rated as the local hero with some of the men on board. Helmuth stopped and talked to them. His hands started to describe maneuvers that must be planes and the two seamen were convulsed at his story.

"Bleeding 'ero! 'E's telling them 'ow 'e shot us down. Bad job we didn't 'ave machine guns or 'e might not be talking so big."

Just as Helmuth finished his story and was about to move along toward Steve and Corky, a bell began to jangle insistently. Helmuth stopped dead, then turned and sprinted for the companionway. He dove down the steep stairs and they could hear his feet clattering at a breakneck pace.

Captain Hansler appeared and shouted for the guards to bring Steve and Corky to him. When they were opposite him, he said:

"Sorry you can't stay on deck, but I don't want you to see how we set up the catapult. However, when it is in readiness for Herr Helmuth, you may come up and watch him take off."

He rapped an order to the seamen in German and turned away as the guards led Steve and Corky below. They waited at the bottom of the companionway. A moment later Helmuth dashed past them and up to the deck. He was wearing Steve's flying outfit and patted the leather and grinned jeeringly at the young American as he passed, saying:

"*Gut, gut, gut.*"

"I guess he means he likes my flying suit," Steve remarked as he watched Helmuth's legs disappear up the companionway.

"Nice of 'im to say so," Corky observed sarcastically.

They could hear shouted orders and the bustle of activity on deck. After what seemed like an eternity because of their anxiety to watch what was going on, the bustle died away and the lieutenant who had been helmsman on the rescue lifeboat poked his head over and called to the guards to bring the prisoners up on deck.

When they came up, they found Helmuth just about ready to climb into the little yellow seaplane. He saluted Captain Hansler smartly and climbed in. The plane rested on a catapult and Steve could feel the vibration of the motors as the vessel swung about to head the catapult into the wind.

In the cabin of the plane, Helmuth waved once. At his signal, the motor roared. He warmed it up while he waited for the vessel to take its position. A wind sock fluttered from a pole at the bow. He watched it closely.

A moment later the wind sock showed that the vessel's position was true and Helmuth waved again. He opened up the motor. It reached a crescendo of power, the triple-bladed propeller bit the air in a silver arc.

Suddenly there was a snap that sounded like a pistol shot. The yellow seaplane hurtled forward, shot off the end of the catapult. It dipped alarmingly and almost touched the waves. Steve's neck ached merely from thinking how Helmuth's neck must have snapped as the plane righted itself and began to climb.

Captain Hansler, Corky and Steve, and the crew, stared after Helmuth as he put the tiny plane higher and higher into the sky. In almost no time at all, it was a rapidly disappearing speck in the sky. Hansler joined them.

"Herr Helmuth will return in a few minutes. Perhaps you had better go below now. Let us say that your exercise period has ended for the time being."

Locked once more in the cabin, Steve turned to Corky.

"Tell me one thing," he begged. "Why is it that Captain Hansler and the doctor and some of the others speak perfect English and that almost all of the men on this tub can speak some English?"

"Hi was wondering habout that myself," Corky observed. "Hi didn't see what flag 'Ansler's flying. Hit might be your Stars and Stripes for all we know, and 'e might be masquerading as a fisherman out of Portland or Boston."

"Say, that might be it! If he's got some way of hiding the derrick and the catapult, maybe he keeps the sailors who can't speak English under cover when he's boarded."

"Look 'ere," Corky exclaimed. "There's our clue —who boarded 'im?"

"Who boarded him?" Steve echoed. "Why—oh-oh! I see what you mean. We've been figuring we were fairly close to the English coast, but maybe we're not. If we were close to England, Hansler and this ship would be under constant watch."

"Hex-actly," Corky said. "The Navy patrols wouldn't let them lay to, the way they've been ever since we came aboard. But if 'Ansler's masquerading as an Hamerican fisherman, why we may be off the Grand Banks."

"And Helmuth could still operate," Steve put in. "Look, the bombers carry wing lights. And they don't fly a straight course for England. If Helmuth took off at about two in the morning and cruised around, he could spot a light—and the rest would be easy."

"Too easy," Corky agreed grimly.

"Still, taking off by catapult at night is a risky proposition." Steve shook his head. "This guy Helmuth must be a pretty good flier, in spite of the fact that Hansler isn't too crazy about him."

" 'Ansler doesn't like 'im because of the job 'e's

doing," Corky guessed, "not because 'e isn't a good flier."

Getting up, Steve went to the porthole and looked out. From far away had come the soft beat of a plane and now it was drawing closer. Steve noticed that the fishing vessel was still headed into the wind, its motors moving just enough to keep it in the same position.

The yellow seaplane appeared high in the sky. It dropped down and circled the ship. He watched it, but Helmuth made his landing out of Steve's range of vision. But this time the plane had sufficient fuel left to taxi slowly over the waves to within fifty feet of the ship. A boat was lowered and the plane towed into position to be lifted aboard by the derrick.

"I wonder what he's been up to?" Steve said turning from the porthole. He perched again on the edge of the bunk and pounded his left palm with his fist. "This is terrible. Here's this guy operating and we're prisoners."

" 'E's operating," Corky amended, "and tonight another flight will be taking off."

"All we can do is talk, talk, talk. We can't stop Helmuth, we can't warn the people at Hatties Field. Steve snorted with disgust. "I've never felt so helpless in my life."

Suddenly Corky raised his hand warningly. Footsteps echoed along the corridor outside. The door opposite theirs opened, but they didn't hear it close. Someone laughed and footsteps crossed the corridor and the key turned in their door. It was opened and Helmuth looked in.

He grinned insultingly at Steve and fingered Steve's flying suit which he was wearing. Helmuth said slowly, *"Sehr gut, sehr gut. Verstehen sie?"*

"What's the bloke trying to tell us?" Corky demanded, pretending not to understand.

"I don't know." Steve looked at Helmuth and shrugged.

"Gut, gut," Helmuth repeated fingering Steve's suit. He made a mocking bow and said in thick English, "Thank you."

" 'E likes your suit," Corky reported.

But Steve had understood and his anger flamed. Seeing that they understood at last, Helmuth laughed again and went out locking the door behind him. They heard him enter his own cabin across the corridor and close the door.

"Hi'd like to scrag 'im," Corky growled. "The blarsted——"

"Wait!" Steve exclaimed softly. "Wait a second, Corky, I think I've got an idea."

"Eh? What is hit?"

"We're going to let Helmuth help us to escape," Steve whispered.

"We're—'ow's that hagain?"

"Come here. I'm going to whisper in your ear, there's just a chance they may have hidden microphones in this room somewhere."

As Steve whispered, a look of amazement spread over the little Corky's face. Then his eyes began to gleam and he grinned and nodded as Steve whispered. But at the end he became very grave.

"Hit's a desperate plan, Steve, a desperate plan."

"I know that, but we're up against a desperate situation," Steve pointed out softly. "Unless we can stop the operation of this ship somehow, it's going to cost the lives of literally hundreds of good pilots."

"Hit's an awrful risk to run," Corky protested.

"We've got to run it just the same," Steve replied. He hesitated and then asked, "Well—are you with me?"

"Up to the 'ilt," Corky said quickly. He patted Steve's arm. "Hi think your plan will work, Stevie, me lad. Hit's just so himpossible and desperate they'll never hexpect hit."

"That's what I'm counting on. Now, let's get some sleep. We go into action at eleven tonight and we must be ready."

VII.

The Wrong Helmuth

ALTHOUGH offered another chance at exercise late in the afternoon, both Corky and Steve begged off on the excuse that they were beginning to feel seasick. Captain Hansler accepted the explanation and warned them that seasickness usually took two forms—violent nausea or terrific sleepiness.

"I guess we've got the sleepy kind," Steve had told him. "We both have been sleeping hard ever since we came down from our turn on deck this morning."

Later in the afternoon, Corky had ransacked the cabin. He had to find or improvise some sort of weapon. Nothing was at hand which they could use. To rip the leg off the cabin's one chair was bound to excite immediate suspicion.

And then Corky had picked the lock on the closet. He came out with a pair of heavy boots. Steve watched him interestedly as Corky stuffed them in a pillowcase. He swung it experimentally.

"Blimey! Has sweet a blackjack as a man could hask."

"Good."

They took a sheet off one of the bunks and remade

66

the bed. While Corky listened at the door so they would not be overheard, Steve tore the sheet into strips. Steve tested the strength of the torn lengths.

"And there we have the lashings," he observed.

From then on they had only to bide their time. But it was hard to wait. Steve tried to sleep, but his plan pounded through his head and made any thought of sleep, or even rest, impossible. Corky, in the bunk above, turned and fidgeted so that Steve knew he too was finding it difficult to wait patiently for the time when they could go into action.

They made themselves eat dinner, which was a repetition of the fish, bread and coffee that had comprised their other meal, but neither of them had any real appetite. The wait seemed interminable.

At about ten o'clock they heard Helmuth enter his cabin across the corridor and shut the door. Steve looked at the luminous dial of his watch. Another whole hour to wait!

He must have dozed off because suddenly Corky was shaking him and whispering, "Hit's time to go, boy."

"Right." Steve sat up and glanced at his watch— it was ten past eleven. "Are you all set?"

"Hi'd blinking well better be," Corky replied grimly.

"Okay. We both know what each of us is to do, so—let's go."

They stole to the door and listened. Steve timed

it. He tapped Corky's shoulder after his watch showed that they had been listening for ten full minutes and no one had passed down the corridor.

Something rattled softly and a moment later the door swung open. Corky reached for Steve's hand in the dark and the young aviator passed him the heavy boots in the pillowcase which was to be a blackjack. Very cautiously they eased into the corridor.

A low light glowed near the companionway. By its dim light they could see that the corridor was empty. Steve closed the door to their cabin and kept watch while Corky crossed to Helmuth's door. He switched the pillowcase to his left hand and tried the doorknob. The door was locked.

Passing the pillowcase-blackjack to Steve, Corky went to work on the lock with his nail file. Helmuth's door opened. Without looking around, Corky stretched back his hand for the blackjack. Steve handed it to him.

Corky held the door ajar until Steve tapped him on the shoulder to signal that the corridor was clear, then he slipped into Helmuth's room. Steve closed the door to their cabin firmly, looked up and down the corridor, and then followed him inside.

They paused a moment just inside Helmuth's cabin. There was no sound outside. They could hear the German aviator breathing deeply.

Stealing up to the bunk, Steve drew a length of

sheet from his pocket and wadded it up in his right hand. Corky stood by Helmuth's head. Steve shifted the wadded sheet to his left hand and stretched out his right to Corky.

Holding hands, Steve with his right and Corky with his left, they stared down at the aviator just barely discernible in the blackness. Steve shook Corky's hand, and counted to himself as Corky returned the pressure, one, two, three, one, two, three, one two, three. That gave them the cadence.

They dropped hands. Still counting at the same pace, Steve said, "One, two, three," to himself. At "three" Corky swung the homemade blackjack with both hands.

Almost at the same moment, Steve leaned forward and jammed the sheeting into Helmuth's mouth as it opened. Corky swung again and Steve grasped the German's right wrist. He couldn't find his left arm.

Before Corky could strike a third time, Helmuth's left arm flew up. Steve seized it and Corky struck at the same instant. Helmuth went limp.

Corky dropped the blackjack and ripped strips of the sheet from his pocket. He bound Helmuth's hands together as Steve held them. The minute that Corky had secured Helmuth's hands, Steve stripped the covers off and bound the pilot's feet while Corky jumped to the door and listened to see if they had attracted any attention.

By the time Steve had lashed Helmuth's feet,

Corky was back. He tapped Steve's shoulders and they changed places silently. Steve took Helmuth's shoulders and Corky his feet. They carried the aviator to the door.

While Steve held him up, Corky opened the door. Steve lugged the man across the corridor and Corky, darting ahead of him, held the door open. Corky went back and closed the door to Helmuth's cabin while Steve hauled the aviator to the bunk and laid him on it. Panting, he sat down on the edge of the bunk.

Corky came in and locked the door to the corridor. He came over and pounded Steve on the shoulder.

"Hit worked. Hit worked like a clock! Steve, you're a blinking genius and no mistake."

"It's worked so far," Steve said trying not to become overconfident at their success, "but we've still got a long way to go."

"We'll do hit, though. We can't fail now."

"Let's tighten his gag and get him in the upper bunk," Steve said, "before I go into my act."

They examined the lashing and secured the gag in Helmuth's mouth. Hoisting him to the upper berth proved to be the hardest part of the job that they had yet faced, but they managed it at last.

When it was done, they stood in the dark and caught their breath. Steve looked at his watch—it was eleven-forty. He whispered:

"Now, tell me what to say again."

"*Ja, ja. Ein augenblick.*"

"*Ja, ja. Ein augenblick,*" Steve parroted.

"Good. Remember, you're angry."

"I will. Well—" Steve held out his hand and Corky clasped it. "Keep punching."

"Good luck and thumbs up," Corky replied.

Going to the door, Steve slid it open. He glanced up and down the corridor and then closed the door behind him. He heard Corky lock it from the inside with his nail file and the sound gave him a sinking sensation in the stomach.

Quickly he crossed the corridor and entered Helmuth's cabin. He snapped the lock and leaned against the door. His heart was pounding. As he leaned there trying to get back his breath, he suddenly remembered that the improvised blackjack was here in Helmuth's cabin.

Should he take it to Corky? Crossing the corridor was risky business, too risky. He searched around until he found the blackjack. He took the shoes out and put them neatly under Helmuth's bunk. But suppose someone noticed that they weren't Helmuth's shoes and got suspicious?

But what else could he do with them? As sure as he tossed them out of the porthole a lookout would hear the splash. He put Helmuth's pillow inside the pillowcase—no one was likely to see that it had two pillowcases.

And now for the waiting.

He sat down on the edge of Helmuth's bunk. He tried to picture what might be going on in Corky's cabin. He wondered how Hugh Gracey was feeling. He looked at his watch. It was two minutes to twelve. This was awful.

Next he tried exploring Helmuth's cabin in the dark. He located the Nazi flier's goggles and helmet and his own flying suit. He looked out of the porthole.

"Steve, you're nuts," he told himself irritably. "You're supposed to be a big boy now—well, act like one."

Determinedly he lay down on the bed and closed his eyes. He fidgeted. He made himself breathe regularly, he forced himself to relax.

Someone was pounding on the cabin door and calling to him. Steve sat up with a jerk. He heard the voice repeat, "Lieutenant Helmuth, Lieutenant Helmuth," as he glanced at his watch. It was ten minutes to two.

"*Ja, ja,*" he shouted.

The man outside said something in German.

"*Ja, ja. Ein Augenblick,*" Steve replied hoping that his answer fitted in with whatever it was the man had said.

He jumped into the flying suit and pulled up the zipper. He pulled on the helmet—it was too big. Why hadn't he tried it on before? Now someone was sure to notice that it didn't fit. What could he do?

He tightened the strap of the goggles and fitted them over his face. That would have to do—he couldn't take any time now. He heard the roar of a plane motor. Good. They were warming it up.

As he stepped into the corridor, he could picture Corky with his ear pressed to the door, listening. Steve was tempted to knock on the door or give Corky some sort of reassuring signal. But a seaman appeared at the end of the corridor. Bracing himself, Steve strode toward him, doing his best to imitate Helmuth's strut.

The seaman saw Steve, waved, and turned. Steve heard his feet clatter on the stairs to the deck. No, not stairs. On a ship you called them—or it—the companionway. He followed.

The noise of the motor told him where the catapult was without his having to look around and thus give himself away. As he walked toward it, a sailor saluted him. Steve saluted back awkwardly, and hurried on.

He took one look at the catapult and the plane standing out boldly under the glare of arc lights. A ladder led up to the cockpit. He forced himself to stroll over. Corky had warned him to take his time, had said nothing was as likely to arouse suspicion as if he hurried too much at any point.

Remembering that, he paused at the foot of the ladder to draw on his gloves. He remembered also to keep his back straight, but he bent over the gloves as though they had suddenly become difficult to get on.

Climbing the ladder, he dropped into the cockpit and pulled the cover shut. He looked down. Faces were turned up to him expectantly. It was a good thing Captain Hansler wasn't down there. Steve had a strong feeling that Hansler would recognize him.

He waved his hand exactly as Helmuth had waved his that afternoon. There was activity below him. Steve fumbled for the throttle. What a break, it was practically the same as on an American plane. He opened it wide.

From the bow fluttered the wind sock. Everything was set. He waved again.

" 'Ave you ever taken orf from a catapult?" Corky had asked when they discussed Steve's plan.

"No, but I'm sure I can make it," Steve had replied.

He wasn't so sure now. He wasn't at all sure. Abruptly the floodlights went off. That was to give his eyes a chance to accustom themselves to darkness. There was a pause.

Someone yelled something at him.

The words meant absolutely nothing. The man yelled again. Steve waved. Nothing happened.

The man yelled again and stared at him questioningly. "Hif you find yourself in a tight corner," Corky had advised, "try and hact like 'Elmuth. Be very 'aughty and such like."

"*Ja, ja!*" Steve screamed and waved impatiently.

Out of the corner of his eye, he saw the man give a signal. The next moment, the plane shot ahead. He was launched.

Steve was so taken by surprise that for a split second he froze to the stick. He saw a moving blackness all around him. Those were waves, and he was slanting down at them.

He eased back slightly on the elevator. The ship didn't seem right. He had no sense of buoyancy. The throttle was wide open and still it didn't seem to help. He almost smacked into a wave. In fact, he could feel it lick at his pontoons.

And then he was flying. He could feel the lift, the plane became an animate object and not a dead weight hurtling through space and subject to the law of gravity. He eased back more and put the plane into a steep climb.

"Better circle the ship," Steve told himself. It was the last thing he wanted to do—gas was going to be precious before he got through with his end of the job. But he did it anyway.

Then he headed a few points south of west.

Looking back over his shoulder, he saw the ship lights go out. It was going to be a trick to find her again—if he got through. He located Helmuth's map case and pulled out a map.

There was a circle drawn in red and when he saw it Steve's heart jumped. If that circle represented the approximate cruising range of Captain Hansler's ship, it was the best luck so far, because it meant Steve was only about five hours straight flight from the American coast!

But that didn't seem right. Why they had flown for at least eight hours before Helmuth pounced on them. But then, he remembered, Hugh Gracey hadn't steered a beeline course—none of the bombers ever did.

The next point was—did the yellow monoplane carry enough fuel to carry him to the coast? He found what he was sure must be the fuel gauge on the instrument panel. He had a full load, but how many flying hours did that mean?

"Guess I'll just have to cross my fingers," he told himself.

As the little yellow plane cut along, Steve was tempted several times to try its guns, but he fought the temptation. This was no time for fooling. When he and Corky had discussed the idea, the one thing that had worried him was—what would happen to Corky and Hugh Gracey when the Nazis realized what had happened?

"Don't worry habout that," Corky had said. "They'll think 'Elmuth cracked up. When they see someone in the hupper bunk, Hi'll tell them it's you—sick as a dog."

Well, that might work for a while—but how long a while?

All that had worried Corky was the risk Steve faced. He was going to look for help. But where was he going to look for it? In the excitement of Helmuth's attack, none of them had thought to check their position. And Hugh Gracey was in no position to tell them that now.

If the red circle on Helmuth's map meant what Steve thought it did, the flight for help was a push-over. But suppose the red circle meant something entirely different? Suppose it marked the position of another Nazi ship, or a good spot for Helmuth to ambush bombers, or—whoa! This was no time for speculation.

"Keep your mind on flying this plane," Steve told himself. "That's all you've got to worry about right now."

Far behind him a thin pencil of light along the horizon told him that dawn was not far off. He dropped down to 500 feet and scanned the thick gray carpet below him for the sign of a ship.

VIII.

The Great Mistake

THE minute hand on Steve's watch was edging up
to twelve and the hour hand was almost over five.
He had watched the thick gray below him turn to
mother-of-pearl, and then pink and rose as the dawn
came up. Now he could see for perhaps five miles
in any direction.

But so far he had sighted nothing.

On and on he roared. And then, far off and a little south of his course, he saw a black thread hanging from the sky. Two minutes later and he knew
that it was not a black thread hanging, but a black
line rising to the sky. A black line that could only
be smoke, the smoke of a vessel.

Steve pointed for it. At ten past five he sighted
the convoy. As he approached, as individual ships
began to take shape, two lean gray destroyers darted
forward. They put themselves a good two miles
ahead of the merchant ships which were traveling in
pairs.

Steve dropped lower. Now he could see pompom guns on the forward deck trained on him.
"That was a good idea," he thought, "always be prepared for the enemy."

Abruptly he realized that they thought he was the enemy!

Oh-oh! He'd forgotten that the lines of the yellow monoplane would label it as Nazi. He was about to waggle his wings, in the hope that would make the destroyers hold their fire, when he realized they might take it as a gesture of defiance.

Even as he thought it, tiny puffs of smoke appeared around the guns. Steve whipped over and darted away. The guns stopped.

He was out of range, but that was no good. He had to get aboard those destroyers. Pushing back the cockpit cover, he fluttered his handkerchief in the slipstream and came in again.

Steve was sure the destroyers must have seen it. But the minute he was in range, the one nearest him opened fire, forcing him to keep his distance. "This is getting silly," he decided angrily.

Doing a half-barrel roll, Steve circled the ship flying upside down. He flew within range and this time the destroyer didn't open fire. But he couldn't land that way.

However, he got close to the ships, close enough to see the look of bewilderment on the faces of the men lining the rails. He fluttered his handkerchief again. An officer raised a megaphone and bawled something at him. Steve shook his head.

The officer with the megaphone turned and conferred with another officer. Steve waved the handkerchief. The officer waved his megaphone. Steve hoped it was an invitation and snapped the plane over.

For one awful second his heart was in his mouth as he saw the gun crew dive to position. But they didn't shoot. He did a wing slip and settled down into the wind. The plane struck a wave and bounced. He hadn't bounced that high the first time he tried a landing.

As he tried for his landing, the two destroyers came about and followed him, their guns trained on the back of his neck. Steve tried it again. He hit and bounced, and bounced again. Then he felt the pontoons glide and knew he was down.

The destroyers closed in on him. An officer leaned over the rail, megaphone in hand, and Steve cut his motor.

"Ahoy, seaplane. Who are you?"

"An American bomber pilot out of Hatties Field. Will you take me aboard?"

"What are you doing in that plane?"

"Take me aboard and I'll tell you," Steve shouted back.

He couldn't hear what the officer said as he turned, but a crew of men jumped to a lifeboat that swung clear in its davits and ready for immediate use. They clambered in and lowered away. Steve climbed out of the cockpit.

When the boat was below him, he hung by his hands from the wing and dropped to the pontoon. He hit and slid off it toward the boat. Two pairs of hands caught him before he reached the water and pulled him inside. The officer was standing in the stern.

"What about the plane?" he asked.

"Leave it here or sink it, I don't care. It's done its bit."

At a command, the sailors dipped their oars, the officer leaned on the tiller, and the lifeboat scudded for the nearest destroyer. As the boat reached the destroyer, a rope ladder was dropped over the side and two of the men caught it.

"Up you go, my lad," said the officer.

"Okay."

Steve climbed up, the ladder pitching with the motion of the gray ship. Two officers were staring down at him curiously. One reached down and helped him up the last few feet. Steve faced the older of the two, and reported:

"I'm Steven Knight, sir, a bomber pilot from Hatties Field. My plane was attacked at dawn yesterday morning and my first officer was wounded. My——"

"What was his name?"

"Hugh Gracey." The older officer raised his eyebrows at the other officer who stood behind Steve consulting a slip of paper. Steve went on, "My radio-man and I decided to follow the plane that attacked us. We——"

"And your radioman's name?"

"Corky Merlin."

Again the older man looked inquiringly at his junior officer. The younger man nodded slightly. Turning to Steve, the old man held out his hand.

"I'm glad to meet you, Mr. Knight. I'm Lieu-tenant Commander Drum and this is Lieutenant Halsey. We'd received a radio message telling us about your disappearance and asking us to be on the lookout for you."

"You seemed pretty suspicious," Steve observed.

"Have to be in this business," Lieutenant Com-mander Drum replied. "We had your descriptions and your names, but I wanted to be sure."

"Where are the other two men?" Lieutenant Hal-sey inquired.

As briefly as he could, Steve sketched in what had happened to them from the time Helmuth attacked to when the destroyer picked him up. The two Royal Navy men listened with mounting excitement.

"Amazing, amazing!" Lieutenant Commander Drum declared. "You Americans are really quite remarkable people, you know. Of course I don't suppose you have any idea of the location of Captain Hansler's *fishing* vessel."

"If I've located myself correctly on this map,"

Steve said hauling Helmuth's map from his thigh pocket, "I can tell you almost exactly where it is."

"By George, this is our lucky day," the skipper cried. "We got one of their subs only an hour ago and now this. Come along, Mr. Knight."

With the destroyer's executive officer at his heels, Steve followed Lieutenant Commander Drum to his "office" where they checked Steve's map against their own. Steve put his finger on Helmuth's map:

"As I figure it out, we ought to be about there."

"How about it, Lieutenant?" the skipper asked.

Lieutenant Halsey measured the spot Steve had pointed out and then turned to his own maps. When he had completed his calculations, he lifted his head from his work, grinning broadly.

"Mr. Knight's correct for all reasonable purposes, sir. He's only out by three miles."

"Out by three miles?" Steve cried. "Does that mean you can't find Hansler's fishing ship?"

"Not at all," Lieutenant Commander Drum replied contentedly. "It means we can't miss them. Let me see that red circle again."

Drum and Halsey bent over Helmuth's map. As they studied it, the officer who had taken Steve off the plane entered. He reported:

"All on board, sir. What shall we do about the plane?"

"Sink her, Mr. Randall, sink her."

"Yes, sir."

As Lieutenant Randall left, the skipper turned to Lieutenant Halsey. "Will you get off a code message and say that pending counter instructions the *Hastings* will join us in hunting down Captain Hansler."

"Very good."

Turning to Steve, Lieutenant Commander Drum announced, "And now, Mr. Knight, while we prepare to go into action, I hope you will allow me to show you how much I appreciate your dropping in on us with the information you brought by having something besides fish and bread for breakfast."

"I certainly could use a decent breakfast," Steve admitted. "I only wish Hugh Gracey and Corky could share it with me."

Glancing at his watch, the skipper remarked, "Breakfast is out of the question, of course. But I rather hope to have them as my guests for a late lunch or afternoon tea."

"No kidding! Say, that'll be swell."

"Yes," the skipper said patting Steve's shoulder and smiling, "it will be—er—very swell. And thanks to you."

It was after two o'clock. Steve stood on the bridge of the *Brookline* with Lieutenant Commander Drum and Lieutenant Halsey. Below them on the deck, he saw Lieutenant Randall, the gunnery officer, looking over the crew of the pompom gun. A feeling of tenseness was in the air.

Two miles off to the left, Steve could see the *Hastings* cutting through the water on a course that paralleled theirs. And about a mile behind, the *Hartland,* another destroyer, trailed them. The three destroyers were advancing in an inverted V formation with the *Brookline* and *Hastings* making the two forward points.

Not even a vestige of smoke betrayed the presence of the convoy, now many miles behind. The three destroyers raced ahead in a grimly businesslike manner that didn't make Captain Hansler's prospects seem very rosy. Drum took his binoculars from his eyes and turned to Steve.

"By the way, we've discovered who Captain Hansler is."

"You have?"

"Yes. He's an ex-Imperial Navy man, commanded one of their subs in the last war. Our people rated him as a first class officer with more successes to his credit than we like to remember, and a reputation for always warning all but armed naval vessels before he opened fire on them. That's more than you can say for some of the Kaiser's submarine commanders."

"Well, then, he's still running true to form. He was swell to Hugh Gracey, and he made Helmuth and another officer leave us alone when they tried to get tough."

"Obviously a gentleman which would make it impossible for him to be a Nazi," Drum observed. "I've met German gentlemen, but never Nazi gentlemen."

"Hansler's a gentleman, all——"

A shout interrupted Steve. Drum glanced through his binoculars and then handed them to Steve without any comment. He pointed a bit to the left and Steve raised the glasses to his eyes.

It was Captain Hansler's ship. There was no mistaking it. How far away it was, Steve couldn't judge, but what had before been a V formed by the three destroyers was now an elongated diamond. Hansler's vessel was about midway between the *Brookline* and the *Hastings*, but much further ahead of them than the *Hartland* was behind them.

As Steve watched, he saw that Captain Hansler's ship was turning away from them. Did that mean he was going to try and make a run for it? And was his unusual vessel equipped with a power plant that was equally unusual?

Suddenly the deck beneath Steve's feet quivered, he felt the destroyer leap forward like a spurred horse. A second later the *Hastings* also stepped up its speed. Behind them, the *Hartland* was rapidly overhauling them. And then Steve realized that the three destroyers were fanning out slightly.

Evidently the maneuver decided Captain Hansler against flight. Instead of turning completely, the mystery ship lumbered along at right angles to their course. The three destroyers veered as they bore down on it.

When they were about a mile away, a set of flags broke out from the mast. A second later Lieutenant Commander Drum spoke softly into the speaking tube. He was answered by a single shot.

As though surprised at the sudden appearance of the destroyers, Captain Hansler's ship hove to slowly. While the *Hartland* and *Hastings* stood off about 800 feet, the *Brookline* sped in until she was within hailing distance. Drum picked up a megaphone. Abruptly he turned to Steve.

"I say, Mr. Knight, crouch down behind the rail, will you? I want your presence to come as a nasty surprise." He called to a man at the foot of the bridge, "Bo'sun! Will you get a cap and coat for Mr. Knight from my cabin?"

"Ahoy, there."

"What do you want?" came an answering shout from the mystery ship.

"Are your parties ready?" Drum asked Lieutenant Halsey.

"Quite ready, sir."

"Very good." Drum raised the megaphone. "I want a look at your papers. We're coming aboard."

"Come ahead," yelled the man on the mystery ship. "But I'm getting good and tired of you limeys running all over this ship a couple of times a day."

"Sorry," Drum shouted brusquely. He turned to Halsey. "Take over while I go aboard. Mr. Knight, are you ready to go along?"

"You bet."

Steve had discarded his flying suit and had on Drum's coat and cap, both of which were too large for him. Drum grinned briefly as he led the way to the deck.

"You're not exactly a perfectly groomed sailor, Knight, but you'll pass. Keep your head down so they can't see your face."

Randall was waiting for them with his eyes dancing. "Think there's likely to be any fun, sir?"

"I hardly imagine so, Mr. Randall."

"That's too bad." Randall glanced over the double rank of armed bluejackets who waited for the order to climb into the lifeboats. He sighed. "That's too bad."

They climbed into the lifeboats and the davits creaked as they were lowered away. Side by side, the two boats were rowed over to the mystery ship. A ladder was lowered over the side for them. Randall drew his service pistol and started up. He was followed by three seamen with submachine guns.

Two men were left to hold the first boat and Drum passed Steve as he prepared to be the first of the second boat to go aboard. He whispered:

"You come up last."

Steve nodded.

One by one, the men in the skipper's boat clambered up the ladder. One of the two men left in the boat told Steve:

"Your turn, sir."

"Thanks."

When he reached the deck, he found most of the crew collected under the watchful eyes of three sailors with submachine guns. A sailor touched his cap to Steve.

"Will you follow me, sir?"

It gave Steve a sense of assurance to see the broad blue back in front of him and the submachine gun the sailor carried cradled in his arms. He was led down to Captain Hansler's cabin. As Steve entered, he heard Drum saying:

"Your papers seem in order, Captain, but what's this story we heard about a pair of our men being aboard?"

"You can look around for yourself, Captain," Hansler replied politely, "but you'll only be wasting your time and ours."

Steve stepped into the cabin and took off Drum's cap. Hansler stared at him without a flicker of recognition as Steve said:

"Hello, Captain Hansler."

"Hansler!" Drum cried. "Why, according to his papers, he is Captain White of Nantucket."

"How's Hugh Gracey?" Steve asked.

"Who is this boy?" Hansler asked the destroyer's commander.

"A recent guest of yours," Lieutenant Commander Drum said quietly. "It's no good, Captain Hansler, we're not going to be fooled this time by your forged papers."

"All right, all right," Hansler snapped angrily, "take me back to port with you and I'll prove who I am. You can even take my first mate. But be a good sport and leave the second mate here so we can get our catch in."

"That's a very creditable imitation of an American accent," Drum said, "but this time we're not only going to take you into port, we're going to sail this tub of yours into dry dock and take it apart."

"What?"

"Oh, yes indeed. In fact," Drum said quietly, "if you'll glance out that porthole, you'll see a prize crew is already on its way here from the other ship."

Hansler made a dive for the drawer of his desk, but Drum lifted the muzzle of the gun he had carried carelessly at his side. He said, "Don't be childish, Captain. A man with your experience must know when it's useless to fight."

"I do." Hansler rose and stretched nervously. In doing so, he managed to peek out of the porthole. "You were serious about that prize crew."

"I certainly was."

"And me?"

"You will return to port on my ship. You and Mr. Knight here, and Gracey and Merlin who are still your prisoners."

"Of course." Captain Hansler turned to Steve and smiled slightly. "Your friend Gracey grew much stronger today. I suspect that he learned of your escape when the little fellow went in to visit him this morning. I wish I had realized then that it was Helmuth I saw in the upper bunk and not you suffering from seasickness. However—" Hansler shrugged, "fortunes of war, I suppose."

Hansler, Lieutenant Commander Drum, Steve and Corky sat in the ward room of the *Brookline*. The ship pitched as she headed back to Halifax, the other two destroyers had returned to the convoy. Drum was saying:

"So there's nothing to worry about in Gracey's condition. He'll pull out of it in no time—and I imagine much of the credit for that must go to Captain Hansler."

"No credit to me," Captain Hansler replied. "I merely treated him as a prisoner of war should be treated."

Abruptly, he glanced up and saw that the three men were looking at him. He flushed. Captain Hansler knew only too well what they were thinking—that very few prisoners of war could hope for decent treatment from anyone serving under the Nazi flag.

To cover the embarrassing pause, Drum asked, "Weren't you operating dangerously close to Canada?"

"No. You see it made our story of being fishermen seem more convincing."

"Yes, but if you were out there to bring down bombers," Steve protested, "I'd think you would want to be nearer England."

"I don't believe you appreciate the range of Helmuth's plane. You see, while the bombers were zigzagging all over the sky in order to avoid being attacked, Helmuth could fly an almost straight course to a likely spot to ambush you. Of course, sometimes he overreached himself—such as yesterday morning when he had barely enough fuel to return on after he shot, or thought he shot, you down."

"He's a good flier," Corky conceded.

"He is if you don't mind his type of work," Hansler admitted. He turned to Drum, "How soon do you expect to be in Halifax?"

"At our present rate, we should make it in about thirty hours or less."

"You could make it in less?"

"Yes, if I didn't give a hang what a burden I threw onto my engines." Drum shook his head. "No, I want to get there with my ship in shape to refuel and put to sea again."

A seaman entered and saluted. He handed Lieutenant Commander Drum a folded sheet of paper.

"This just came in, sir. Lieutenant Halsey decoded it and asked me to say he'd be right down, sir."

"Be right down?" Drum looked puzzled as he took the paper. He said, "Thank you," to the sailor and opened the paper. He glanced at Corky, Hansler and Steve. "Excuse me, will you? I imagine this must be rather important."

Unconsciously all three watched him as he read the radio message. The sailor stood close beside him. There was no sign of expression on Drum's face as he finished reading. He looked up impassively and gazed at Corky and Steve, and then reread the message.

Just as he finished, Lieutenant Halsey entered the cabin with a pistol in his hand. Behind him stood two sailors with submachine guns. Steve looked at them with surprise and then glanced quickly at Hansler.

"'As something gone wrong, Captain?" Corky asked.

"I'm afraid so."

Captain Hansler sat quietly, waiting with complete stoicism for whatever was to happen. Steve glanced at him and then asked Lieutenant Commander Drum:

"Does it concern Captain Hansler?"

"No." Lieutenant Commander Drum got slowly to his feet. He repeated, "No. As a matter of fact, it concerns you, Gracey and Merlin."

"Concerns us?" Corky burst out. He looked at the armed sailors. "Captain! What's happened?"

Hansler looked up in surprise and Drum said, "Suppose I read you the message I have just received from my commanding officer."

Everyone watched Lieutenant Commander Drum as he spread out the radio message. There was such absolute silence that when he cleared his throat the sound seemed unnaturally loud. The skipper said:

"I shan't bore you with the salutation. The message reads: 'Put Gracey, Merlin and Knight in irons. Prepare to bind them over to PBY flying boat within one hour. Radio when transfer has been made. Send Hansler with them and return to convoy duty.'"

"Put us in hirons," Corky cried. "What's the matter with the bloke? Don't 'e know we're bleeding 'eroes?"

"I don't understand it myself," Drum admitted, "but I must obey orders."

"Someone's made a mistake, a great mistake," Steve said. "It—they must have made a mistake."

IX.

Trial for Treachery

IN IRONS, their faces grave and puzzled, Steve Knight and Corky Merlin leaned on the rail of the pitching destroyer and stared to the West from where, at any moment, would appear the PBY flying boat that was to return them to Canada. Neither Steve nor Corky spoke. What was there to say? Both were positive that some awful mistake had been made—at least, that was what Corky had insisted to Steve.

At last Steve turned from the rail and went to where Hugh Gracey lay in a stretcher on the deck. Hugh's eyes burned peculiarly in his pallid face as he studied the young American flier. He said softly:

"Sit down, Steve. And don't take it so hard."

"How else can I take it?" Steve demanded dully. "I thought we did a pretty good job—and they're arresting us."

"I know. Everything looks pretty black at the moment, but let me ask you something."

"What?"

"Why did you run the risks you did when you took off in Helmuth's plane and went for help?"

"I was trying to do what I considered my duty."

"Right. Well, remember this, youngster—when you serve duty, you must take what comes."

"I don't get it. What do you mean, anyway?"

"It takes courage to do your duty as you see it. Sometimes it's physical courage and sometimes it's mental and moral courage. I—I may not have a chance to talk to you again without interruption," Gracey went on, "and I just want to remind you that the road of duty leads to many strange places, it calls for many sacrifices."

"I know it calls for sacrifices," Steve protested sullenly.

"Sometimes, it even calls for the sacrifice—temporarily at least—of our friends. But—" Gracey sighed, "duty comes first."

"All right, all right. Duty comes first. I still don't get what you're driving at," Steve growled. "All I know is that you and Corky and I took it on the chin. So what happens? We get slapped into these things."

He rattled his wrists inside the handcuffs. Gracey was about to reply when Corky turned from the rail.

" 'Ere 'e comes," he announced dispiritedly. "The blooming jailers coming for hus."

Well down in the western sky, a dot was turning rapidly into a plane as the PBY's motors dragged it through the air. Steve got up and joined Corky at the rail and they watched it drawing closer and closer. Almost reluctantly, Corky said:

"Look 'ere, Steve, just keep a stiff upper lip. And remember, everything will be hall right in the end."

"What's got into you and Hugh," Steve complained. "Why the sermons all of a sudden? And another thing, both of you guys act as though you were sorry for me. Why me? We're all in it—whatever it turns out to be."

"Well, you see," Corky began hesitantly, but he was interrupted by the arrival of Lieutenant Commander Drum.

"Gentlemen, I've allowed you a bit more freedom than my orders indicated, probably a good deal more than the Admiralty would approve of, but I feel sure a mistake has been made." He turned and shielded his eyes to watch the flying boat a minute before he faced them again. "I only hope that everything turns out satisfactorily. And, although it's a little out of order, please let me know of anything I can do or say to help you in any way."

"Thank you, sir," Hugh Gracey said from his stretcher. He lay with his hands folded over his eyes to keep the sun out of them. "I think everything will turn out all right."

"Yes, thank you," Steve echoed. As he turned to the rail, he muttered, "I wish I were sure about things turning out all right."

The PBY was less than a quarter of a mile away. On the bridge, Lieutenant Halsey ordered the destroyer to a stop while Lieutenant Randall had a boat's crew piped on deck. The *Brookline* lost way and the flying boat circled her once and then slid to a graceful landing. A hatch went up and a man in flying helmet stuck his head out.

"Ahoy the destroyer. Have you got my prisoners?"

"And just who might you be?" Drum shouted back coldly.

"It's all right, sir," the flier replied. "I have an order for them and everything's shipshape."

"I'll just have a look at that order before I turn these men over to you," Lieutenant Commander Drum called. He turned to his gunnery officer. "Mr. Randall, row over and get me those orders."

"Very good, sir."

As Randall and his crew lowered the boat, Steve asked, "You think the orders might be phony?"

"Mr. Knight, I don't think anything. But I do know this—the orders strike me as absolutely insane. If it should turn out that I had handed you over to an enemy plane masquerading as one of ours, I'd never forgive myself."

"An enemy plane?"

"Yes. You see I can think of no earthly reason why our people should want you arrested. But I can think of any number of reasons why the other side might like to get their hands on you and at the same time rescue Captain Hansler. In these days, it pays to be safe first so that you needn't be sorry later on."

Randall's lifeboat had returned and now one of its crew was climbing the ladder. He stepped up to Drum and saluted, and handed the skipper a sealed envelope.

Breaking it open, Lieutenant Commander Drum's eyes went immediately to the signature. Satisfied on that score, he read the orders carefully. When he had finished, he followed the orders and slipped them into his pocket.

"Gentlemen, the orders are genuine and I have no alternative but to turn you over to Lieutenant Nesbitt in charge of the flying boat. However," his tone was entirely sincere, "I still believe a serious mistake has been made and I shall be only too glad to do anything in my power to bring that to the attention of the proper authorities."

"Thank you," Steve said.

"Now—good luck, gentlemen." Lieutenant Commander Drum summoned Lieutenant Halsey from the bridge. "Mr. Halsey, will you take over."

Under Halsey's directions, Hugh Gracey was lowered to the lifeboat. Steve and Corky were sent down after him. They waited while two guards went to bring Captain Hansler from the brig in which he had been confined following the radio message. Hansler climbed down the ladder and joined them in the boat, but made no attempt at conversation.

Steve was surprised at the philosophical way in which Hansler accepted his fate. But at that, he thought, it's easier for him. He knows what's in store for him—he'll be a prisoner of war and well treated. The trouble with this whole deal is that Hugh, Corky and I don't know what this is all about.

The lifeboat pulled over to the PBY and Steve, Corky and Captain Hansler were sent aboard. The crew was very careful in transferring Hugh Gracey's stretcher to the flying boat. It was difficult to arrange space in the crowded cabin so that Hugh would be comfortable, but it seemed to Steve that Lieutenant Nesbitt made very little effort to do so. In fact, Nesbitt's jauntiness had annoyed him from the moment the flier had stuck out his head and bawled for his prisoners.

"You won't be very comfortable," Nesbitt told Hugh Gracey, "but I don't know that it matters very much."

"You mean it's a short hop?" Steve asked.

"I mean nothing of the sort," Nesbitt replied shortly. He turned his back to Steve and his eyes met Hugh Gracey's understandingly. Gracey nodded very slightly, and Nesbitt said, "I really can't feel very much sympathy for you fellows. Especially you and Merlin, Mr. Gracey."

"I'm sorry you feel that way," Hugh said evenly.

"Do you mind telling us why we were put in irons?"

"I'd mind very much," Nesbitt replied.

Steve felt himself growing hot, but he fought down his anger. There was nothing to do but sit tight and await developments. Lieutenant Nesbitt closed the hatch and tapped his pilot on the shoulder. The motors roared to life and the flying boat skipped away from the destroyer.

For a moment the pilot studied the drift of the destroyer's smoke and then turned the plane to head her into the wind. Steve stared at the faces of men lining the destroyer's rail—to a man they looked glum and suspicious.

A moment later he realized that he was looking down at the destroyer. A good man, the pilot of the PBY—he'd taken off without even Steve knowing it. He tensed as he waited to see in which direction the plane headed. And then the sun glared into his eyes and he knew they were flying west.

That meant Lieutenant Commander Drum's faint suspicion that this might be a ruse was unfounded. They were not in the hands of the enemy. But it also meant that they very definitely were under arrest.

There was very little conversation on the flight to the flying boat's base. What little there was seemed designed to make Steve dislike Lieutenant Nesbitt still more. The man seemed to go out of his way to be irritating. By the time the plane slid down to the calm waters of the harbor and taxied to the dock, Steve found himself hating Nesbitt very sincerely. Their parting did nothing to correct his feeling of antagonism.

"Well, here we are," Nesbitt said gaily as they reached the seaplane dock. "And now I can turn my jailbirds over to their guards and fumigate my plane."

"Fumigate yourself," Steve snapped.

"I wonder if you'll be quite so cocky by the time they get through with you," Nesbitt asked calmly. "Out you go, the guards are waiting for you."

Nesbitt followed Steve and Corky to the dock where he saluted a lieutenant who was in charge of a detail of armed sailors.

"Here are your prisoners, Lieutenant. Better send a couple of men in for the other fellow, he's on a stretcher. I don't know whether he's sick, sullen, or sulking."

"Why, you—" Steve began, but the lieutenant cut in:

"Silence from the prisoners."

He sent in men to carry Hugh Gracey out and Steve saw that his first officer was biting his lips because of the carelessness with which he was being handled. He'd have protested, but Corky sensed his reaction and nudged him.

Single file, with a guard on either side, they were

led off through the yard and taken to an old brick building with heavily barred windows. Steve and Corky were put in a cell together while Captain Hansler was placed in an empty cell further down the row. As Corky sat down dejectedly, Steve watched the jailer lock their door.

So this was what it was like to be put in jail? Well, he didn't like it—not one bit. Steve had a sick feeling in the pit of his stomach. There was a terrible mistake somewhere. But would the mistake be found out?

Corky just sat on the bunk staring at nothing. Evidently, he didn't feel like talking. Steve didn't blame him for that, but on the other hand, he wanted desperately to talk—to anyone, about anything. Even if he could only find out what had happened to Hugh.

When the jailer brought them food at seven o'clock, Steve tried to get some information from him, but the man didn't reply to his questions. He refused even to answer when Steve asked about Gracey.

"Hugh's probably hall right," Corky grunted. "Put 'im in the 'orspital, that's what they did with 'im."

"Well, then, why didn't the jailer say so?" Steve flared. "There's no law against his answering questions like that is there?"

"Hi don't know," Corky growled, and devoted

himself to eating the beans, meat, bread and coffee that had been brought them. At least, it was a great deal more palatable than the fare they had received on Captain Hansler's mystery ship.

At eight, footsteps resounded along the cell block and a detail of bluejackets marched up. The Lieutenant in charge ordered them out and they were marched away, this time without Hansler.

"No sense in asking where we're going," Steve said to himself, "they won't tell us a thing."

They were marched outside and again wound their way across the yard. The red brick building to which they were taken was partially covered with ivy and looked as though it had been built in Colonial days. They were led inside and taken to a large room paneled in dark oak. A long table ran down the middle of the room. Steve and Corky were seated in chairs about six feet from the table.

A moment later Hugh Gracey was wheeled into the room in an invalid chair and placed beside them. He looked at them and smiled without much amusement. The presence of guards behind them discouraged any conversation.

Outside in the hallway, someone barked an order and there was the measured cadence of men coming to attention. The door opened and a group of officers, both in army and navy uniforms, entered and filed slowly to places at the table. Steve noticed that Major Jeff Sears was among them, but the major did not look at him. In fact, it seemed to Steve that he made a studious effort to avoid his eye.

An officer came over and stood in front of Steve, Corky and Hugh. "I have been delegated by the Court to act as your counsel. Is there anything you care to say that may make my job a little less distasteful?"

"Court?" Steve gasped. "What are we on trial for?"

"You will learn that when you hear the charges read, if you don't know already. Anything you care to say?"

"Not until I know what we're charged with," Hugh Gracey said.

"That goes for me, too," Steve volunteered.

"Me, too," Corky Merlin echoed.

"Very well. However, if after you have heard the charge you care to make a statement, I shall be glad to transmit it to the Court or the Judge Advocate as the case may be."

With a curt nod, the officer returned to his place at the table. The admiral sitting at the head of the table rapped and called the Court to order. He directed a warrant officer to read the charge.

It was all pretty much of a blur to Steve. Somewhere along the line he heard his name mentioned. He caught the words "deliberate treachery" and "sabotage" and heard something about "consorting and relaying information to the enemy in an effort to hinder and hamper the activities of the Royal Navy."

When the charges had been read, the officer nearest them ordered Steve, Corky, and Hugh Gracey to stand.   They obeyed.

"Are you guilty or not guilty?" demanded the admiral.

"Not guilty," they chorused.

"Sit down," the officer ordered under his breath.

The strain of standing even for a moment had told on Hugh and he almost collapsed.   No attention was paid to his condition.   From there on the proceedings became a nightmare.

Looking back on it later, Steve remembered that Hugh had been wheeled up to the table first, to be cross-examined by the admiral and other officers comprising the Court.

Had Gracey given information to the enemy? He had not.   Had he consorted with the enemy in any manner? He had not.   How was it, then, that the Consolidated had been so far off his course?   Hugh did not know.

A map was unrolled and Hugh was asked to point out, to the best of his ability, the spot at which they had landed.   Hugh had to hoist himself out of his wheel chair to lean over the table and do so.

That was the spot, was it?   Hugh said it was. That was completely off the course, was it not? Hugh admitted that it was.   How had the bomber gotten so far off its course? Hugh did not know.

A piece of paper was held out to Hugh and he was asked if the note bore his signature. Hugh admitted that it did. The note was then unfolded and he was asked to whom he had written it.

"I didn't write that note, sir."

"You ask the Court to believe that, although you admit the signature is yours, you did not write the balance of the note?"

"I do, sir."

"Can you explain how your name might be attached to such a note?"

But Hugh could not. And after a few more questions, he was wheeled back to his place beside Steve and Corky. Steve wanted desperately to know what was in the note, but he didn't dare whisper.

Corky was summoned to the table. He was asked virtually the same questions that Hugh had been asked. His replies were the same. He, too, was puzzled by the fact that they were so far off their course.

Why hadn't Corky radioed for help when, as they claimed, they were attacked by an enemy seaplane? Corky had been too busy trying to help Gracey. It was his job to radio for help in case of an emergency, was it not? It was. Then why had not he done so? Corky was stumped, and floundered badly.

Corky, too, was shown a piece of paper and asked to identify his signature. He admitted the signature was his.   He was shown the rest of the note and, as had Hugh, denied that he had written or had anything to do with its being written.   He was told to sit down.

Now it was Steve's turn.

As he stepped up to the table, Major Jeff Sears rose and went to the head of the table where he whispered in the admiral's ear.   Steve stood uncomfortably at the table while the eyes of the officers at it bored into his.   After a moment, Major Sears returned to his place.   The admiral cleared his throat.

"Gentlemen, it has been suggested that the Court excuse Steven Knight on several counts.   In the first place, his arrival at Hatties Field was almost a matter of minutes before he took off on the flight.   He had no time in which to become a party to the act of treachery committed.   Secondly, he comes with the highest personal recommendation of any officer of the United States Navy."

"Does that recommendation satisfy the Judge Advocate?" asked one of the officers.

"It does," the admiral declared with finality.   "As a third point, Major Sears advances the theory—and it seems reasonable—that young Knight was the innocent dupe of more experienced fliers.   It is moved he be dismissed."

"I wasn't duped," Steve broke out.   "If Hugh and Corky are guilty of anything, then I'm just as guilty as they are."

"Silence, please."

"I don't know what those letters, or notes, or whatever they are say, but I know Corky and Hugh are just as true to your country as you are. Maybe more so for all I know," Steve stormed. "Hugh got himself all shot up—does that look like he was consorting with the enemy? And Corky picked the locks that made it possible for me to escape from Hansler's ship and then stayed behind to take the rap when they found out I was gone. Does that look like treachery?"

"While the Court honors your sentiments," the admiral said in a tone that silenced Steve's outburst, "it feels itself in a better position to judge the merits of this case than you are. We appreciate your courage, Knight, and believe that you acted in good faith at all times."

The admiral looked along the table for confirmation. Each officer nodded agreement.

"Steve Knight is released from custody by this Court and given his freedom with the Court's apologies for any embarrassment or anxiety it may have caused him."

"I don't want my freedom," Steve cried, "unless you free Hugh and Corky as well."

"The Court has made its decision in your case."

"I was in command of that bomber. If we were away off our course or anything else went wrong, it was my responsibility. You can't take it out on these men, I'm the guy to blame, I'm the guy to——"

"Major Sears," the admiral barked, "you will escort Mr. Knight to new quarters."

Sears came over to Steve, took him by the arm and tried to lead him away, but Steve was still full of fight. All he cared was that his friends were being unjustly accused and it was up to him to stick by them. But this was a court-martial and he wasn't given a chance.

At a nod from Sears, two sailors came over and pulled Steve from the room while Major Sears followed. They took him outside and closed the door. Major Sears led him along to the sea wall.

"Sit down a minute, Steve, and cool off," Sears suggested. "Besides, I'd like to talk this over with you."

"What's there to talk about? Somebody's railroading Hugh and Corky right up before a firing squad."

"I don't believe it's quite that bad."

"All right, they're railroading them out of the service and into jail for the duration of the war and getting them disgraced. It's that bad, isn't it?"

"Yes," Major Sears admitted slowly, "it is that bad."

"Then what is there for us to talk about? You didn't do anything to help Corky and Hugh, so that means you're against them. Well, I'm for them and I don't want anything to do with their enemies."

Sears watched the angry young man beside him from the corner of his eyes. Then he took out a cigarette and lighted it. He smoked thoughtfully for a moment in silence.

"Steve, did it ever occur to you that Merlin and Gracey might be traitors?"

"It did not!" Wheeling on Major Sears, Steve said hotly, "It did not—and I'll tell you why."

Briefly he recounted their experiences after the take-off from Hatties Field. Major Sears listened gravely. Steve finished up:

"Do those men sound like traitors? If they were playing around with the enemy, do you think Hugh would have been wounded? They're being rail-roaded, I tell you."

"I admire the way you stick by your friends."

"Can you tell me any good reason why I shouldn't stick to them? The only thing those officers have against them is a note, or a couple of notes. All right, if those notes are so damning, tell me what they said."

"I'll admit the notes weren't conclusive evidence," Sears confessed.

"What did they say? Tell me what they said?"

"I—I'm sorry, but I can't do that."

"You can't brand those men as traitors unless you back it up by telling me what the notes said. Do you think they got a fair trial?"

"I don't care to answer that question. I will admit, however, that I know of a personal enmity between Captain Grannell and Hugh Gracey."

"Which one was Grannell?"

"He's the admiral's aide."

"Oh-oh! You know that and you think they got a fair trial? You *know* they're being railroaded and it's up to you to do something."

"I don't believe it is," Sears remarked coldly.

"Then I will!" Steve burst out. "I'll go over the admiral's head, I'll go right up the line until I get Corky and Hugh a fair trial."

"That's entirely up to you. You are a citizen of a friendly nation, the Court has exonerated you, and——"

"The Court exonerated me? Wasn't that nice of it," Steve muttered sarcastically. "It didn't seem to me they gave me much credit. Can I go on flying bombers?"

"No. Under the circumstances, I hardly believe you would be acceptable."

"Now let me see if I've got this straight," Steve said slowly. "I was a dupe and am not suspected of treachery. You're not going to run me out of the country, but you don't trust me enough to let me continue flying for you. Isn't that about the way it stacks up?"

"Well—er—yes. You are substantially correct."

"All right, then I'll tell you what I'm going to do. I'm going to stick right here and work to get Hugh and Corky a fair trial, and I'll keep on working until I get them out or you people bounce me out of Canada."

"That, of course, is your privilege. But let me remind you, Steve, there's a war going on."

"Meaning exactly what?"

"I mean that there has been plenty of treachery from a number of different sources. It appears that this isn't entirely a war of one nation against another —it's a war where people who believe in Naziism, whatever their nationality, are fighting people who believe in freedom."

"I'm not worried about that," Steve replied. "All that worries me is getting Hugh and Corky a fair trial."

"Very good." Major Jeff Sears rose. "If you will report to our headquarters in Montreal, you will be given a month's pay."

"I wouldn't take a dime from—" Steve stopped. He realized that he had no money of his own and would have expenses while he worked for Hugh and Corky. "Thank you."

"A plane leaves for Montreal in the morning. I will give you a pass. Now, if you will come with me, I'll take you to your quarters."

In silence they left the sea wall and crossed the

yard to a wooden barracks. Major Sears said something to a petty officer on duty and left Steve with a curt good night.

"Come with me," the petty officer said brusquely. Steve was uncomfortably aware that he had omitted the usual "sir" and that his whole tone was contemptuous. Obviously, he was regarded with as much suspicion and contempt as Hugh and Corky.

For a long time, Steve tossed restlessly in the bed to which he had been assigned. He was in a cubbyhole of a room and there was no one to know his bitter unhappiness at the way things had turned out. That was a break, anyway.

X.

A Blow for Freedom

ARMED with a pass on the plane to Montreal sent him by Major Jeff Sears, Steve breakfasted and roamed the yard waiting for take-off time. No one greeted him and he was aware of being watched. There was no mistake about it—freed or not, he was in disgrace. And then he saw the newspaper.

It was lying where someone had tossed it away. Steve picked up the paper and the headline jumped out at him: *Bomber Crew Found Guilty*. The story named Steve, Hugh and Corky as traitors and retold what had happened during the court-martial. Steve threw it away angrily. Probably every paper in Canada and the United States had called him a traitor by now.

In some ways, he decided, Corky and Hugh Gracey were better off. They didn't have everyone avoid them and refuse to meet their eyes. He might as well be in the cell with them.

He went over to the field long before it was time for the plane to leave. Again he was treated to suspicious side glances and complete silence. He was in disgrace and no mistake.

When at last it was time for the take-off, he climbed in the plane. His pass was accepted without comment and no one spoke to him at any time during the trip.

Arriving at Montreal, he was the last one to leave the plane. He hoped no one would look at him— and he got his wish. But as he walked over to take a bus for Montreal proper, he was aware that people were talking behind his back. Steve seethed inwardly.

Leaving the bus station in Montreal, he took a taxi to the office where he was to be paid. He was greeted coldly by the man behind the desk the moment he told his name.

"Steve Knight? Oh, yes. Come in."

Steve went into a private office and was introduced to the manager of the bank. The manager drew back his hand when he heard Steve's name and told him curtly to sit down.

"Of course you know you can have a check on any bank in the United States if you wish."

"I know, but I'd rather have the cash."

"Aren't you returning to the States?"

Steve said he wasn't and the manager's eyebrows raised. However, he paid Steve off with twenty fifty-dollar bills. He made no attempt to bid Steve goodby.

For an hour or so, Steve wandered aimlessly through the streets of Montreal. He was wondering what he should do first. And how about Lieutenant Commander Drum? The skipper of the *Brookline* had promised to do anything in his power to help them.

That was the ticket—he'd get in touch with Drum. But how? He set off for St. Catherine Street. A nondescript man in a blue suit and wearing a gray hat followed him at a distance of about twenty-five feet.

Reaching St. Catherine Street, he called a taxi.

"Take me to the local headquarters of the Navy," he directed.

More on instinct than anything else, he glanced out of the back window. A man with a gray hat and blue suit was hailing a taxi as he drove away from the curb. Funny the man should stick in his mind. He was sure he'd seen him somewhere before. Oh yes! He'd been looking in a shop window and Steve, staring up at an old French church, had bumped squarely into him.

And here he was again!

After explaining his wants to several clerks and being shunted from one to another, Steve was ushered into the presence of an elderly man wearing the stripes of a lieutenant commander. Steve explained that he wanted, at his own expense, to send a message to Lieutenant Commander Drum.

"Drum, eh? Man on active duty?"

"Yes, sir."

"Hmmm.   What is your name?"

"Steven Knight."

"Knight, Knight," the officer mused.   He consulted a memorandum and his eyes became unfriendly.   "Sorry.   Impossible.   Good day."

"But you don't understand, sir.   Lieutenant Commander Drum knows the truth of a certain situation and wants to help my friends and———"

"Nothing more to say.   It is impossible for you to communicate with Drum in any way.   Good day."

To end the interview, the officer busied himself with the correspondence on his desk.   Sick with anger and disappointment, Steve turned and left the office.   He wandered up to St. Catherine Street again and stumbled along.

From time to time, he stopped to look into store windows.   But actually, he saw nothing that was on display.   His mind was busy with the problem of freeing Hugh and Corky.   And behind him wandered a man in a blue suit who wore a gray hat, a nondescript little man who never let Steve out of his sight.

Long after lunch hour Steve realized he was hungry.   He glanced around and saw a small restaurant that looked inviting.   As he entered it, the man in the blue suit dashed a few doors down the street and went into a phone booth.

Steve found that the menu was printed in French. He studied it, but it was no use, he didn't understand a word of it. He had to ask the waiter to translate. The waiter's translation was almost as hard to understand as the printed menu.

However, the food needed no translation—it was delicious. Steve had just finished his soup and was halfway through his fish, when a man paused beside his table. Steve glanced up to find the man smiling down at him.

"Monsieur, I beg your pardon, but do you mind if I sit at this table?"

It seemed a slightly strange request, there were plenty of empty places in the restaurant, but the man who was tall, middle-aged, and well-dressed, seemed very pleasant. Steve shrugged.

"No, of course not."

"Let me explain and then I shall not bother you again," the man said as he seated himself opposite Steve. "You see, this is my favorite restaurant and this is my favorite table and the waiter is also my favorite waiter. There—I shall not bore you further."

"Not at all," Steve assured him, "perfectly all right."

He continued eating in silence, his mind busy with his problem. The man opposite him greeted the waiter affectionately and ordered in French. The waiter bowed and scraped and seemed mightily impressed by his presence.

From then on, the man opposite Steve did not

speak, but there was a difference between his silence and the silence the young flier had been experiencing the last day and a half. This man seemed friendly. His silence seemed the result of consideration and not because he thought Steve was a traitor. And Steve was very lonely.

"Nice town you have here," he remarked awkwardly as the waiter brought his dessert.

"Ah, you like Montreal? It is a beautiful city. Have you never visited her before?"

"No, this is my first trip."

"What a pity. Have you visited perhaps Quebec?"

"No."

"Ah, but you should. It is then even more French than Montreal." The man pronounced Montreal as though it were spelled Mon Rayal. He went on, "If I can be of assistance to you, Monsieur, please call on me."

He handed Steve a neatly engraved card and lapsed again into silence. Steve looked at the card and read: Raoul Haye Chambert. He studied it as he ate, again conscious that Chambert's silence was one of friendly consideration.

As he signaled for the check, Steve tapped the card. "Thanks for your card, Mr. Chambert, maybe I'll take you up on your offer."

"But, of course, Monsieur. Please feel free to telephone me at any time, you will find my name in the book. And how are you called?"

"I'm sorry. My name's Knight, Steve Knight."

"Thank you, Monsieur Knight." As the waiter brought the check, Chambert waved him away. "Monsieur Knight is my guest."

"Merci, Monsieur Chambert." The waiter bowed himself away.

"No, look here, you mustn't pay my check," Steve protested.

"Monsieur, you are a visitor to my city. I insist that you accept my hospitality. Now—where do you stay, at what hotel?"

"I haven't gone to a hotel yet," Steve explained. "I only arrived this morning."

"Capital! Then you must stay with me as my guest."

"No, I can't put you to any trouble."

"It is no trouble, I assure you," Chambert protested. "You are an American. I want you to think well of *les Canadiens*."

"*Les Canadiens?*" Steve repeated.

"Yes. You see, I am French. I call myself and my people *les Canadiens* because they, too, are French. We are not English."

"But you all live under the British flag," Steve said.

Chambert shrugged. "Perhaps you are right, but I can assure you that the British have not been as friendly to us as they should have been. No, we have many grievances against them."

"Well, they haven't given me the best break in the world," Steve said—and then kicked himself for talking out of turn.

"Ah, then you know," Chambert said wisely. "These British, they are not fair to me and my people."

"Don't they let you vote?" Steve asked.

"Oh yes, we can vote. But what good is voting?"

"Why that's how you keep democracy," Steve protested. "As long as you have free elections, no one can take your freedom away."

"Perhaps, but we have not been treated well, my people and me." Chambert rose and held out his hand. "Monsieur, this has been a most fortunate meeting. If you will not permit me to put you up as my guest, perhaps you will have dinner with me tomorrow."

"Say, that's darn nice of you. I'd like to very much."

"*Bien.*" Chambert picked up his card and took an expensive fountain pen from his pocket. He scribbled an address on the card. "I shall expect you then at seven o'clock. Good day, Monsieur Knight."

"I'll be there," Steve promised. "So long."

Chambert strode off, a tall, erect man in carefully tailored clothes. Steve picked up his hat and followed more slowly. He was amused at the respect with which he was treated by the waiter and the proprietor.

As Chambert reached the street, he made an almost imperceptible signal to a man leaning against a lamp post, a man who wore a blue suit and gray hat. The man nodded slightly and moved further down the street. A moment later Steve appeared. He looked up and down the street and then started off toward the center of town. He did not see the man in the blue suit fall into step some way behind him.

The meeting with Raoul Haye Chambert had done much to restore Steve's spirits. Chambert didn't know he was disgraced. Furthermore, from what the French Canadian said, he too had suffered at the hands of the English. That made a bond between them.

Steve spent the afternoon finding a hotel and buying pajamas, tooth brush, and other minor accessories. He was dead sure he'd never return to Hatties Field for his bag.

After dinner that night, he picked out a list of names from the telephone book. He had the name of the ranking Naval officer, the ranking Army officer, and the leading newspaper publishers. If the Army and the Navy wouldn't listen to his story, perhaps the newspapers would.

Returning to his hotel, he picked up the key to his room. On the point of turning away from the desk, he had an idea. He asked the room clerk:

"Ever hear of a guy in this town named Chambert?"

"There are lots of Chamberts," the clerk replied. "You don't mean Raoul Haye Chambert, by any chance, do you?"

"Yes, he's the one. What's he famous for?"

"Oh not much," the clerk replied with feigned casualness. "He's only the richest or second richest man in Canada. Why?"

"I was just wondering," Steve replied cautiously. "I heard the name somewhere and wondered who he was."

"Quite a colorful character," the room clerk volunteered. "He's got a huge estate up around Murray Bay somewhere and owns a bunch of mines in northern Ontario and steel mills and—well," the clerk sighed enviously, "anyway, he won't starve."

"Doesn't sound as though he would."

"Just the same, he claimed he would once." The clerk chuckled at the memory. "Just after the war started and the Government tried to clamp down on excess profits, old Chambert let out an awful howl. Said the Government was trying to ruin him because he was a French Canadian, said they were trying to starve him and a lot of stuff like that."

"What happened?"

"Nothing. Just the usual bickering back and forth." The clerk snorted, "You could tax that fellow every day and he'd still have plenty."

Nodding absently, Steve said good night and went up to his room. He had taken a small one because he didn't know how long the fight for Hugh and Corky's freedom would last. If it hadn't been that he was determined to do everything in his power to free them, he would never have accepted a cent, even though he was entitled to it under the contract he had signed with Major Jeff Sears. He didn't want the King's shilling—only it was a thousand bucks in this case—if he didn't deliver the King's bomber.

But the main thing, the only thing that counted, was to free Hugh and Corky, to clear them and himself of the stigma of failure and treachery that clung to them as a result of their disastrous flight.

He dropped off to sleep wondering how he was going to accomplish what looked like a pretty hopeless task.

A good night's sleep was even more stimulating than his meeting with Raoul Chambert. Steve started out to see the Army and Navy officers full of confidence and determination. That was at eight in the morning.

At noon he returned to the hotel, crushed. His pleadings had been in vain; he had met a cold impersonal wall of rebuff. Nothing he had said changed the minds of either of the two ranking officers that Corky and Hugh deserved another trial. Worst of all, both seemed completely indifferent to whatever fate befell Hugh and Corky.

His success with two newspaper publishers had

been equally bad. Neither of them were interested in Hugh and Corky, nor worried about their disgrace. Never, Steve was thinking, had he met such a cold-blooded crew in his life.

But now what was he to do? Well, Ottawa was the capital. The only thing to do was to go to Ottawa and go on fighting. What had that big American newspaper man said? Oh, yes. "Those who have fought for a good cause and lost need only ask themselves—when do we fight again." That was all right for Heywood Broun to have said, but Steve was considerably younger and he was sullen and resentful of the attitude he had met.

But he'd go to Ottawa and continue the fight. In fact, he'd call off his date with Chambert and go down that very afternoon. He phoned the desk and asked for the next train to Ottawa.

"There's one leaving in an hour and twenty-five minutes," the clerk told him, "and another at four-ten."

"I'll catch the next one," Steve replied. "That's at two-fifty-five."

"Yes, sir."

"Thanks."

Hanging up, Steve tossed his things into the small handbag he'd bought the previous day. Maybe he'd have better luck in Ottawa. Oh-oh! He'd almost forgotten—he must call Chambert and break his date for dinner. He went to the phone and asked the girl to get him Mr. Raoul Haye Chambert. He hung up and continued packing.

A moment later the phone rang. Steve answered.

"Mr. Knight, this is the desk clerk. I'm sorry about that call you wanted to make. Something has happened to the system and it's being repaired. There will be no calls going through outside the hotel for at least a half-hour."

"Well," Steve thought a moment, "I guess it doesn't matter. I just wanted to break a date, but I can call from the station."

"If service is continued within the next fifteen minutes, shall I call you, sir?"

"No, I'll phone from the station. Thanks."

Hanging up again, Steve crossed the room and slumped in a chair. He had an hour and twenty-five minutes to kill.

In the room next door to Steve's, a man in a blue suit took off a pair of earphones and turned to the man who sat beside him. He jerked his thumb toward Steve's room.

"He was going to call the boss, but something's wrong with the phones. No outgoing calls."

"Yeah, but what's this stuff about train service to Ottawa?" his companion demanded. He hauled a tattered time table from his pocket and scanned it.

"That's what I thought. There's a train in twenty minutes. Why did the clerk tell him the 2:55 was the next one?"

"How should I know?" demanded the man in the blue suit.

"Think there's something funny going on?"

"Aw, don't be silly," the blue-suited man growled. "That dumb clerk was too lazy to use his eyes. Hop outside to a phone booth and tell the boss that Knight is going to break his dinner date. He's going down to Ottawa."

"I hope you're right about that clerk being lazy," the other said doubtfully as he rose. "It would be pretty tough if he was hooked up with British Intelligence."

"Go on, scram! You're worse than an old woman."

Half an hour later there was a knock on Steve's door. He got up and opened it. Major Jeff Sears stood outside.

"May I come in for a moment, Knight?"

"Why sure, sure." Steve's face lighted up. "Say, is everything all right. Are they giving Hugh and Corky another trial?"

"Knight, I have some very bad news for you."

"Bad news?" Steve faltered.

"I flew down here this morning and was told that you had been to see several important people. You left your address, you know."

"Yes, I know."

"I have come to tell you that your efforts in your friends behalf are of no use."

"But, Major, they've got to be. They deserve a fair trial and I'm going down to Ottawa to try and get it for them."

"You must postpone your trip to Ottawa. It will get you nothing."

"I'm going. They deserve———"

"Knight, you can't help Gracey and Merlin now."

"Wha-what do you mean?"

"They were executed by a firing squad at eight o'clock this morning."

The room spun. Steve staggered back and dropped down on the edge of the bed. He stared unbelievingly at Major Sears. The army man stared back at him coldly. Steve gasped:

"You mean—Hugh and Corky were shot? This morning?"

"Exactly."

"But, Major! Why—why that's murder. How could you do it?"

"I don't quite agree with you."

"You mean you think they deserved to—to die?"

"I do."

With a bound Steve was off the bed. He jumped at Sears, his fists flying blindly. He cursed Sears and struck at him wildly. Sears parried the attack, but made no effort to counter any of Steve's blows.

When some of Steve's fury was spent, Major Sears pushed him away. He said coldly, "I might repeat that I believe they deserved their fate."

"You murderer, you murderer. I'll make you pay for this, you dirty killer."

"We shall see."

Wheeling, Major Sears marched from the room and slammed the door behind him. Steve slumped down on the bed and made no attempt to stop the dry, racking sobs that convulsed him. They'd killed Hugh and Corky. Sears had murdered them. He'd gotten Steve set free. Why hadn't he gotten Hugh and Corky a fair trial?

XI.

The Hunting Grounds

THE phone rang. Steve got up wearily and went to it. As he picked it up, he noticed absently that it was late afternoon. He said, "Hello?" and a pleasant voice at the other end of the wire said:

"I beg your pardon, but this is Raoul Chambert. Are you by any chance the Steve Knight I met yesterday?"

"Yes."

"But how fortunate! Monsieur Knight, I was in the hotel, I happened to glance over the register and I saw your name. Ah-ha, I said to myself, perhaps that is my young friend of yesterday. I shall see. This is a most happy accident."

"Yes."

"Good, I am glad—but you do not sound happy. Is everything well with you?"

"No."

"No? I am desolated to hear that. Come, I am downstairs now, at the desk. You must come home with me right now."

"I—let's skip dinner tonight, Mr. Chambert. Some other——"

"No. I insist. Let me cheer you up." As Steve started to protest, Chambert said with mock severity, "Either you will come down at once or I shall come up to your room and drag you out by the scruff of the neck. That is an embarrassing prospect, no?"

There was no use pretending, Steve welcomed the prospect of friendliness. He relented. A few minutes later he stepped out of the elevator into the lobby. Raoul Chambert came to meet him, hand outstretched and smiling sympathetically.

He shook Steve's hand warmly and then piloted him outside to his car. The chauffeur jumped out and held the door for them. They drove off. And Chambert was wise enough to make no attempt at conversation.

Picking up the speaking tube, he directed the chauffeur to drive them up the mountain before taking them home. Then he sat back and waited.

But the view of Montreal stretched beneath him did nothing to lighten the depression that weighed on Steve. The bitterness that had resulted from Major Sears' news of the execution remained. Only now that bitterness was growing and it was being directed more and more at Sears. The whole thing was becoming a personal issue.

They drove to Chambert's home. It was one of the show places of North America, but Steve was in no mood to notice or appreciate its luxury and beauty. He sat in a period chair and stared moodily at the empty fireplace completely oblivious of the mantel which had come from a famous chateau in France.

"My friend, you are sad," Chambert said softly. "I sense in you that a great wrong, a great injustice has been done you. Can I help in any way?"

"It's too late for help now."

"Perhaps, perhaps not. I am at your disposal."

Little by little Chambert drew out Steve's story. How he had come to Canada to fly bombers to England, about meeting Hugh Gracey and Corky Merlin and liking them immediately, about the trip and Helmuth's attack. He told about Captain Hansler, the escape, and the rescue. And then he told about the court-martial—and its result.

"Don't you see?" Chambert asked when Steve had finished. "They have vent their spite on your friends. They would have done so to you, but you are an American citizen."

"I don't see what you mean."

"But it is so obvious. This Sears, I have met him. All he cares about is getting bombers to England. Very well. You failed. What then? Then he hates you and your two unfortunate friends. He has them shot."

"You think Sears is responsible?"

"But of course! He managed to have you turned free because of your citizenship and because you were recommended to him by an officer in the United

States Navy. He does not dare touch you. But your friends—ah, that is another matter."

"I knew he had me released," Steve agreed slowly, "but I didn't think he was solely responsible for the —execution."

"Ah, but I know the man. He thinks of but one thing—get the bombers to England. If you fail, he will find some excuse to have you done away with. It has happened before."

"Then he should be kicked out of his job. He should be exposed."

"Quite true."

"Look, Mr. Chambert, you're a big shot. Will you help me to get Sears broken?"

"My dear Steve, in the interest of justice I should like nothing better, but I am helpless. These British—" He shrugged expressively. "It is true as you say, I am a 'big shot,' but does anyone listen to me? No. My voice carries no more weight than the mouthings of a farmer or a laborer."

"But surely—" Steve began, but Chambert went on bitterly:

"It is of no use. I have tried to reason with the Government but to no avail. I make a proposal to the Government and they refuse me. 'No, no,' they say, 'what you propose is not democratic.' They pursue a will o' the wisp and call it democracy."

"But you've got to preserve democracy," Steve

protested. "Why it means freedom and justice for people."

"Of course," Chambert said hastily. "I love democracy. I believe in it. But one must be practical. Here they are, they are losing the war, but still they will not be practical."

"You think they're losing it?" Steve asked incredulously.

"But of course. Very well, if they will not deal with the victor—" Chambert stopped abruptly as he saw Steve's expression. He went on smoothly, "How can they win when they permit a man like this Major Sears to give orders?"

"I don't think you're right about their losing," Steve said.

"I mean they must lose unless they get rid of Sears and all the men like him," Chambert explained. Steve relaxed and he went on, "You do not know, but there are many men like Major Sears. Something must be done to break their power or all we people, people like you and me, Steve, who love democracy, will be defeated."

"Yes, but what can we do?"

"Ah, there I have a plan."

"You have?"

"But, yes. However, you would not like it because unless you are very clever you might think that it would not help."

"I'd like to know what it is."

"And I would like to tell you," Chambert replied, "but I am afraid you are too young, too inexperienced. You would jump to the wrong conclusions."

"I guess I'm pretty inexperienced," Steve admitted, "but I wouldn't jump to conclusions."

"It is a very daring and desperate plan," Chambert continued, "but it must be both daring and desperate to succeed. I wish I could tell you because you, Steve, could be of great help."

"I could?"

"But certainly. You could help all people who love democracy and, at the same time, repay Major Sears for what he did to your friends."

Steve jumped to his feet and clutched Chambert's arm. "Listen," he said tensely, "I'm in on anything that will help democracy and bust Sears at the same time. I don't care what it is."

"Ah, but you would misunderstand, you would not be able to see behind the immediate results."

"No, I wouldn't," Steve declared positively. "I want revenge. I want to fix Sears for all time. And if I can help the people at the same time—fine."

"I don't quite know whether to trust you."

"You can trust me, I swear you can."

"Suppose my plan brought about the death of some innocent men? How would you feel then?"

Steve swallowed. "Corky and Hugh Gracey were innocent men."

"And their deaths," Chambert pointed out, "were supposed to help along a cause."

"That's true. I hadn't thought of that."

"Then you think that the deaths of other innocent men might be justified?"

"Yes. I do."

Chambert's eyes glittered. He rose quickly and turned so that Steve couldn't see his face. He pulled a bell cord and ordered the servant who appeared immediately to have dinner served. When he turned back to Steve, his face was again pleasant and friendly.

"Steve, I am putting my life in your hands—I will tell you my plan."

"You will?" Chambert nodded gravely. "When?"

"Tonight. Immediately after dinner. But," Chambert warned, "but not here."

"Not here?" Steve puzzled.

"No. We shall fly to the lodge I maintain in my private hunting grounds. Shall we go in to dinner?"

Throughout the sumptuous dinner that followed, Raoul Chambert was witty and interesting. Steve might have been embarrassed by the two servants who waited on them and anticipated every wish and by the elaborateness of the food and the service, but Chambert kept up a steady flow of conversation. He put Steve entirely at his ease.

After dinner Chambert took Steve to still another room, the "Brown Room," where coffee and cognac

were served before a fire.   Steve refused the addition
of cognac to his coffee and for the first time Chambert
raised his eyebrows.

"What about your plan?" Steve asked eagerly as
they finished their coffee.   "You said you'd tell me."

"And I shall."   Chambert summoned a servant and
ordered his own flying suit and one "for Monsieur
Knight."

A servant helped Steve to climb into a flying suit
made of suede as soft and pliable as silk and lined
with thick warm beaver.   Steve had never seen such
luxurious flying clothes.   Chambert, attired in an
even finer suit, led Steve out on a terrace and across
a broad stretch of lawn to a garage.

But the building turned out to be not a garage but
a hangar.   Two mechanics opened the doors at their
approach and a man in a liveried flying suit saluted
Chambert respectfully as they entered.   Steve saw a
five-place monoplane gleaming in the low lights.

"Here, turn on the light," Chambert ordered.
"Monsieur Knight is a flier.   He will enjoy examining my plane."

Although Steve did not recognize the make, he
saw at a glance that Chambert's plane combined
speed and luxury—and plenty of each.   It was liquid-
cooled and would, he guessed, deliver close to 18,000
horsepower.

"And now we fly," Chambert announced before

Steve had made more than a preliminary examination, "to my hunting grounds."

Eagerly Steve climbed into the plane. He would have preferred to sit with the pilot, but Chambert waved him to the comfortable back seat. They taxied out of the hangar and shot off down the lawn in the dazzling glare of floodlights.

Steve was surprised by the comparative silence of the motor. He was surprised also by the speed with which the floodlights were switched off. They climbed in a slow tight spiral directly above Chambert's estate, as nearly as Steve could judge, and at about 15,000 feet leveled off and headed across the city.

After some minutes of silence, Steve remarked, "Mr. Chambert, you said something about my being able to help you."

"Yes. Did you notice my pilot-chauffeur?"

"Not especially. Why?"

"He is an excellent flier, but he is not a young man any more. He lacks courage and initiative. Those qualities I feel you possess in abundance."

"Yes, but how does that fit in with your plan? What is your plan?"

"Wait until we have reached my hunting grounds."

If Steve had not been so depressed, if the thought of Corky and Hugh's execution had not been gnawing at him, he might have noticed the sadistic gleam that came to Chambert's eyes as he rolled the phrase "my hunting ground" over his tongue. But he did not notice.

However, he did notice that the roar of the plane's motor had suddenly increased tremendously. Chambert must have equipped it with some form of muffling device. Steve wondered idly what speed they were making.

And suddenly he was also aware that they had left Chambert's estate a long time ago. Just how long, he had no way of knowing. He kicked himself for not looking at his watch. He did so now, and Chambert noticing the gesture said:

"We should arrive in perhaps twenty minutes. You have enjoyed our trip?"

"Very much," Steve said, "but how far are we going?"

"Over 800 air miles," Chambert replied with satisfaction, "and it takes us less than three hours."

"Say, that's good time. That means almost 300 miles an hour."

"Much better than that. You forget that we climbed with snail-like slowness so that the noise of our plane need not disturb the slumbers of the British." Chambert laughed heartily. "My plane can make better than 400 miles an hour at 10,000 feet."

"Not bad," Steve admitted admiringly. "I didn't realize your lodge was so far away."

"My hunting grounds," and again Steve failed to hear the subtle emphasis Chambert gave to the words, "are less than ninety minutes flight from Hatties Camp."

"Good hunting up there?" asked Steve innocently.

"I hope to have excellent hunting," Chambert replied tensely.

The roar of the motor diminished sharply and Steve realized that they were coming down. He'd like a chance to examine that motor more thoroughly, he thought, and then stared at the darkness below to try and spot a landing field.

But the ground below was an unbroken stretch of blackness. Had it been light, Steve's eyes would have seen an uninhabited country with patches of natural meadow dotting a carpet of forest land.

The plane began a series of slow turns at a speed Steve guessed to be very close to the stalling point. Suddenly floodlights swept across a field below them. The pilot did a quick wind slip and landed sharply. It wasn't a good landing from the standpoint of smoothness, but Steve realized that it was a masterly one from the standpoint of getting them out of the air and on the ground in an absolute minimum of time.

Almost before the pilot had applied the brakes to end their run, the lights went out. Men swarmed around the plane and Chambert opened the door and motioned Steve to alight.

"These are my hunting grounds," he purred.

Two lights winked on, outlining windows of a house. As Steve followed Chambert toward it, he could hear the plane being pushed to its hangar by the ground crew. Chambert led him up on a porch and more lights went on. A door was opened for them and they entered a huge, two-story living room which peculiarly enough managed to exude an air of luxury despite its artfully crude log walls, floor, and ceiling.

While the servants in his Montreal home had worn a plum-colored livery, Steve found that Chambert had dressed those in his lodge in green. Oriental rugs struck an incongruous note against the log floor, highly waxed though the logs were.

Five-foot logs crackled in a wide fireplace. Chambert went to it and kicked the end of a log as he unzipped his flying suit. Steve slipped out of his and sat down on the long sofa that faced the fire. He was conscious of a growing excitement—he was going to hear the plan, at last he was going to hear the plan. He waited tensely.

Leaning his shoulder against the mantel, Chambert half turned to face Steve. He studied the young flier a moment before asking:

"Do you like Major Sears any better now than you did this afternoon?"

"I hate Sears," Steve growled. "I hate him."

XII.

The "Reasonable" Plan

A COFFEE table was set up before the fire by one green-clad servant while another brought in a huge tray with coffee, fragile china, and sandwiches. Steve was half aware that both servants looked pretty tough and that they served awkwardly as though unused to the work they were doing. Chambert poured coffee for Steve and himself.

"So you still hate Major Sears?"

"Why shouldn't I?" Steve demanded aggressively. "He's a killer."

"And you would like to discredit Sears?"

"I'd like nothing better."

"What do you think would happen to him if four or five bombers were lost from every flight that set out for England?"

"It would make Sears look pretty incompetent."

"Suppose even more than five bombers were lost?"

"I imagine Sears would be taken off the assignment."

"And that," said Chambert, "is exactly my plan."

"Yes, but the loss of planes will only bring Sears' transfer. I want to see him disgraced like I was—or shot like Hugh and Corky."

"I think I can arrange that part for you, if you will help me take care of the other part."

"That's a deal. But why do you want to shoot down bombers?"

"Well that part is a bit difficult to explain," Chambert said smoothly. "You see, *mon ami,* this war is being conducted all wrong. To save the lives of thousands of men, a hundred men, perhaps two hundred must lose their lives. But isn't it better to sacrifice a few than many?"

Steve agreed that it sounded reasonable.

"I have begged and pleaded with the British to no avail—only when they lose men and machines will they be willing to listen to me." Chambert watched Steve as he added, "Remember, I warned you that you might not understand the value of my plan."

"That's right," Steve agreed. "Only when you talk about shooting down five or six planes in every twelve-plane flight—well, I hate the thought of it for one thing, and I wonder if the loss of planes may not so cripple the English that they'll lose the war."

"Which would you prefer, to save the lives of a few men and lose the lives of many? Or to shoot down, perhaps with your own hand, a few men in order that innocent men, thousands and thousands of them, might be spared?"

"I'd rather shoot down the few men even if I had to do it myself."

"Of course! Because you are a man with heart, because you hate war. I honor you for your choice, Monsieur." Chambert saluted Steve with his upraised coffee cup. "You are a flier and know little of politics and statecraft. I ask you to trust me, follow me blindly if necessary, and I will help you achieve your personal revenge on Sears and at the same time help the whole world back to peace."

"That sounds great."

"And you are with me? Even when you may not understand the reason for my actions?"

"I'm your man, Mr. Chambert."

"Good." Chambert rose and held out his hand. "Welcome to my cause. Tomorrow, you become the commander of all my air force."

"Your air force?"

"Yes. I have twelve interceptors and thirty-six bombers stored in secret hangars on the grounds. Unfortunately, I have only fifteen pilots and none of them have had your training or experience. That, you understand, is why you are so necessary to my success."

"Say, maybe I could teach them some of the stuff they don't know."

"That is exactly what I had in mind."

"So I'm the commander," Steve remarked.

Chambert saluted him smartly. "Colonel Knight, I have the honor to greet you. My compliments, sir."

Colonel Knight. It sounded pretty good to Steve's ears. He certainly had come up in a hurry.

"Tomorrow will be a very busy day," Chambert declared. "I suggest, Colonel, that we get as much sleep as we can."

"Very good, sir."

Chambert summoned a servant. "Conduct Colonel Knight to his quarters. Colonel, you will find pajamas and everything you need waiting for you. Good night, sir."

"Good night."

Steve and Chambert exchanged salutes and the young flier left the room. Chambert smiled slyly at his departing back.

Sunlight was streaming in his bedroom as a knock on the door roused Steve from deep sleep. He called out "Come on in," and a green-clad servant entered bearing a small breakfast tray. He placed the tray on the table beside Steve's bed and saluted.

"Did Monsieur le Colonel sleep well?"

"Perfectly, thanks."

"Monsieur Chambert awaits you at your convenience, sir."

"My compliments to Mr. Chambert and tell him that I will join him within twenty minutes."

Steve beat his estimate by almost five minutes. He found Chambert standing on the broad porch drinking in the salty pine-drenched air that swept in from the Gulf of St. Lawrence. It was a beautiful morning, and Steve, true to his training, noticed immediately that it was a perfect day for flying with a steady, not too strong wind coming in from the southeast.

"Good morning, Colonel." Chambert clicked his heels.

"Good morning."

"You have thought well of what I told you last night? And your decision is——?"

"My decision is unchanged. I'm with you."

"*Bien!* Come, we visit now the hangars and then I will introduce you to the men of your command."

Very conscious of his responsibility, Steve fished a stub of a pencil and an old envelope from his pocket as they went down the steps into the first hangar. He noticed that the hangar had been blasted out of solid rock.

"How do you get the plane to the surface?"

Chambert showed Steve an elevator arrangement and the young flier got quite a shock as he realized that it was the twin of one he had seen in Honduras. However, the one down there had been built by von Rein, the head of Nazi secret operations in Central America. It was sheer coincidence that this hoist— and the hangar itself—resembled it.

Six interceptors were housed to a hangar. Steve got his second shock as he saw them. They were Messerschmitts, there was no mistaking those square wing tips. He turned to Chambert.

"But these are German planes."

"But of course!" Chambert seemed honestly amazed at Steve's surprise. "Look you, Steve, I have important friends. They were able to secure for me twelve Messerschmitt fighters and thirty-six Stuka dive bombers."

"They got them for you?"

"Surely. All these planes have been shot down in action with the R.A.F. and my men have reconditioned them. I defy you to find so much as a scratch or a spot of oil on them. You will swear that they are practically new though not as modern as the planes now in use."

"Shot down by the R.A.F., eh?"

"Yes. And remember, Colonel, it was important that I get German planes—my plan demands German planes."

As Chambert had said, the planes were in perfect condition. Not only the fighters, sheltered in six different hangars, but also the bombers—which were housed three to a hangar—appeared as though they had never had more than a brief test hop. Steve was delighted. The condition of the planes proved that Chambert's mechanics knew their stuff.

By the time they had completed their inspection of eighteen hangars, Steve was delighted with the set-up. While he would have preferred English or American ships because of their better quality and design, Chambert's air force was the equal of any in the air.

His admiration of the hangars, their safety against attack, and the way they had been concealed was outspoken.

"Yes, I was fortunate in being able to secure the services of—of French contractors to build my hangars. And you are pleased?"

"The whole thing is immense. Why say, Mr. Chambert, you could bomb New York from this base, I'll bet. You could get down and back and never be found."

"Ah, but who would want to bomb New York?" Chambert laughed heartily at the thought. "What a quaint idea. Now I will introduce you to your men. Of them, I am not so proud."

"Why not?"

"Well you see, Colonel, I had to take what I could get. None of them has had any training in military flying. And many of them, I regret to admit, are men who used to fly liquor to your country during Prohibition."

"They sound like a tough crew."

"They are, but they are loyal to me which is all I ask."

Chambert took Steve into a pine grove where he discovered a low lodge so built and placed that it was invisible from the air and even difficult to spot from the ground. It was comfortably fitted out—a large living room occupied one side of the building while individual bedrooms were on the other side. Six men were grouped about a table playing poker as they entered. Seeing them, one of the men leaped to his feet and blew a whistle.

Nine other men spilled into the living room from the bedroom section and lined up with the poker players who were already standing at attention. Chambert smiled benignly.

"At ease, men. This is Colonel Knight who will be in command of squadron. You will accept his orders and obey him as though I were speaking."

As Chambert instructed them, Steve looked his fliers over. They were a tough lot all right. Roughly, they divided into two groups—those between the ages of nineteen and twenty-five and those between thirty-six and forty-five. A motley crew with only one trait in common—toughness.

"Colonel Knight, allow me to introduce your second-in-command, Captain Fr—Fred Smith."

A few of the men snickered as a tall blond man stepped forward and, after saluting, held out his hand to Steve.

"Welcome to the squadron, Colonel Knight."

"Thanks. I'd like to talk to you about what training the men have received."

"I am at your command, Colonel."

"Perhaps that can be done after lunch," Chambert suggested. "Report at one-thirty, Captain."

"Yes, sir."

On their way back to the lodge, Chambert remarked, "They are not much to look at, my men, but they are all fine fighters and very tough.   That is a good thing, is it not?"

"Yes," Steve agreed slowly, "the only trouble is that sometimes men who are tough fight well only when they're winning, and fold up when the breaks go against them."

Two days of intensive training followed Steve's talk with Captain Smith.   He found that all of the men were excellent pilots and the three who handled pursuit ships were good at dogfighting.   The flight was divided into three pursuit ships and six bombers. Had the bombardiers of the bomber detail been as expert in bombing practice as they were with machine guns, Steve would have had a squadron to reckon with.

They were quick to catch on to the rudiments of formation flying and the cooperation necessary between bombers and fighters on a joint attack mission. Steve and the squadron flew for several hours both morning and afternoon and not once did they sight another plane or a ship that might report their presence.   Chambert had stressed the need for secrecy and before each practice flight his own monoplane took to the air while the chauffeur kept watch.

As they finished up their workout the afternoon of the second day and had landed, Chambert's chauffeur strolled over to Steve who was climbing out of his flying clothes while he waited for his Schmitt to be stored in the hangar.

"You're all right, son," the chauffeur declared. "You know this racket backward."

"Thanks, Eddie. Why doesn't Mr. Chambert let you join the squadron?"

Eddie laughed shortly. "He doesn't trust me."

"He doesn't trust you," the young American stammered. "I don't get it."

"No? Okay, make out like I didn't say anything."

"Yes, but what do you mean?" Steve pressed.

"I wish I'd learn to keep my big mouth shut," Eddie groaned. He looked at Steve shrewdly a second. "Ask Chambert why he doesn't let me fly with his pack of wolves. And if you don't like his answer, tell him what I said."

"Do you want me to tell him what you said?"

"That's up to yourself, my friend. It won't do me any good, but I don't guess very much more can happen to me. So long."

Steve watched the flier walk away. As he stared after him, Captain Smith sidled over to him. He nodded toward Eddie's retreating back.

"What is on his mind?"

"He thinks we're pretty good," Steve said.

"Was that all he thought?" Smith asked.

"Yeah. I asked him why he didn't fly with us and he said Mr. Chambert needed him too much." Steve sighed. "He's a good man and we could use him."

"That is true." Smith saluted. "Good day, Colonel."

"We'll try that bombing formation again tomorrow morning," Steve said. "See you then."

Walking back to the lodge where Chambert had given him quarters, Steve wondered about Eddie and his remark. Why didn't Chambert trust him? The chauffeur looked as tough as any of the men in the squadron, but there was some subtle difference that Steve couldn't put his finger on. Eddie's speech marked him as coming from the United States, and Steve had come to realize that many of his men were foreigners with a very limited command of English. Even Captain Smith's speech was too precise for English to be his native tongue.

So Chambert didn't trust Eddie. He trusted Eddie enough to have him as his aerial chauffeur, but he didn't trust him enough to let him join the squadron. The puzzle jogged Steve's imagination.

He planned to ask Chambert about it at dinner that night, but the French Canadian had news of his own. He was beaming as Steve sat down across the table from him.

"Colonel, I have had marvelous news. An old friend of mine—a fellow countryman of yours as it happens—is coming to visit us. He will be a great help in our plans."

"Swell."

"But yes. I received word from him this afternoon. I hope he is pleased with the progress the squadron has made under your leadership."

"I certainly hope he is. Is he a flier?"

"He is everything, my dear Colonel. A man of many talents."

"That's fine. We'll do our—" Suddenly a thought hit Steve. "Say, how did you hear from him? Have you got a radio?"

"Radio? No. I have no radio here. You have seen that for yourself." It seemed to Steve that the man was stalling, but he wasn't positive. Chambert went on, "No, a fisherman came over by motorboat from Washikuti Bay with the news. There is a telegraph office in the lumber company office there."

"Oh. Say, you ought to have a radio up here."

"Colonel, you are right," Chambert agreed heartily. As he probed all the advantages of having a radio station, Steve's mind jumped.

Chambert had said that a fisherman came over from Washikuti Bay in a motorboat. Eddie was supposed to be on patrol against just such a situation; he was supposed to warn them at the approach of anything or anyone who might betray their operations. Eddie had given no warning. He had allowed a motorboat to sail by which meant the fisherman must surely have seen their maneuvers.

Did that really mean that Eddie was, as he declared, not to be trusted? Or did it mean that Chambert had lied?

A radio on the hunting grounds? There were a thousand spots where a fully equipped station could be maintained without Steve's knowledge. Chambert said that he had been over the place. He had, but not to the extent that Chambert implied. And the people who had built the hangars were capable of building a still more secret building for the radio set.

"By the way," he said carelessly, "I asked Eddie how he'd like to join the squadron."

"You did? And what did Eddie say?"

"He said he didn't think you could spare him. But I certainly could use him, Mr. Chambert, and I could use ten or twenty more like him."

"Yes, Eddie is a fine pilot." It seemed to Steve that Chambert's tenseness at the mention of Eddie had gone. "But I need him myself, Colonel, he is important to me."

"Okay," Steve said, and added casually, "Maybe I can borrow him some time."

XIII.

The Boil-Over

IT WAS impossible for Steve to sleep. He tossed on his bed as fragments of his conversations with Chambert whirled through his mind. The more he thought about it, the more loose ends began to appear. Chambert had a plan, a most reasonable plan. The plan would bring sure defeat to the Nazis—so Chambert declared. But would it?

So far, the meager details Chambert had given Steve seemed more likely to help the Nazis. In his blind determination for revenge on Major Jeff Sears, Steve realized he had swallowed Chambert's ideas without examining them properly. What had he gotten into? Had——

Something scratched softly on his door.

Steve listened a moment and then rolled over on his side. Was Chambert a Nazi? That didn't seem reasonable, he was French and the French were hereditary enemies of the Germans.

Again he heard that faint scratching.

Rising silently, Steve tiptoed to the door. He turned the key gently. He turned the knob and swung back the door. A man was crouched by the door. As the door opened, the man hissed warn- ingly. He stood up and entered Steve's room.

"It's me. Eddie," he whispered as Steve closed the door. "Listen, I got to talk to you."

"What about?" Steve demanded brusquely.

"I got a question to ask you and I want a straight answer."

"You have, eh?" In the darkness Steve was aware that Eddie held himself stiffly and his right arm was crooked at his side. Chambert's airplane chauffeur held a gun. Steve snapped, "Well, ask it."

"Are you a Nazi?"

"Me? A Nazi?" Steve saw Eddie's right arm start to rise. He stalled, "What do you want to know for?"

"Don't stall me," Eddie growled. "Give it to me straight and give it to me quick. I'm not playing."

So this was it. A sudden recklessness gripped Steve. He'd messed up everything, but no more— from here on he was awake and flying under his true colors. He bunched himself, prepared to jump at the man with the gun.

"I'm no Nazi," he barked and was about to spring, hoping to get his hands on Eddie before the gun went off.

"Good." Eddie straightened up and his arm fell to his side. "Good."

Steve caught himself. Was this a trick? His voice was suspicious as he asked, "Why do you think that's good?"

"Listen, kid, I didn't think you were a Nazi like Chambert and the rest of them, but I couldn't figure it."

"Then Chambert is a Nazi?"

"Of course he is. Say, are you trying to kid me?"

"No, but—" Steve hesitated. "But if Chambert's a Nazi and you aren't, why are you hooked up with him?"

"I might ask you the same question," Eddie pointed out grimly. "My reason is that Chambert is giving me protection from—well, never mind why. He's giving me protection. He knows I'll go along with him, I got to go along with him. But he also knows I can't stomach this Nazi stuff. That's why I told you he doesn't trust me."

"Are you sure he's a Nazi?"

"I'm plenty sure. Come on and I'll show you something I just found."

Slipping into some clothes, Steve followed Eddie out into the hall. He locked the bedroom door carefully and they stole along the hall and down the stairs. Eddie led the way back through the kitchen and out into the chilly night.

They dodged along from tree to tree until they were out of sight of the house. Then Eddie cut through a pine grove with Steve at his side. As they walked silently along, the aerial chauffeur said:

"Imagine, I been coming up to this place for months and only tonight I located this place."

"What place?" Steve whispered.

"A short wave radio station."

"That reminds me. Did you see a fishing boat come over from Washikuti Bay this afternoon while I was maneuvering with the squadron?"

"A fishing boat? No. What makes you think one came over?"

"I don't think so, but Chambert told me that's how he received the news of the arrival of a friend of his."

"He's kidding you. He got it over this radio of his. Now take it easy, we're almost there."

Flitting from tree to tree, Eddie led him forward. Suddenly the chauffeur stopped and gripped Steve's arm. He pointed ahead. Steve saw nothing. They waited in the shadow of a spruce.

A familiar aroma reached Steve's nostrils—coffee. Someone was brewing coffee in the blackness ahead. But there was nothing there!

And then in the nothingness ahead, Steve heard the unmistakable rattle of cups. As he strained eyes and ears, he heard a sudden crackle. Cups thumped on saucers and he heard the scrape of feet on boards. Two men spoke in low tones for a moment and then the crackle was tuned out and became the soft pulsating of a dance band. A man was singing, but in what language he was unable to tell.

At the end of the song the radio was snapped off. Suddenly a light appeared in the darkness ahead and it outlined a man's body. He whistled softly and called, "Ludwig, Ludwig," to someone in the darkness.

Steve and Eddie froze. Again the man in the lighted doorway called. From not more than a hundred feet behind them, someone replied, *"Ich komm"* and a dead twig snapped as a heavy foot stepped on it. Steve melted into the spruce boughs pulling Eddie after him.

A man walked slowly through the grove. He seemed to be looking from side to side. Steve could feel Eddie tremble. They were both thinking the same thing—that man had been in the grove as they came through.

The man passed them. For a moment he was outlined against the lighted door before he went inside. The door closed and the light vanished. Again there seemed to be emptiness ahead. Eddie sighed.

Steve shook himself. He whispered, "Let's get out of here." His knees felt weak. But before he could move, the door opened again.

This time three men came out. Slowly and purposely they separated until they were about twenty feet apart. They walked into the grove in which Steve and Eddie were hidden by the sweeping boughs of a spruce.

"They're after us," Eddie breathed.

There was no mistaking the fact that the three men were looking for someone. Evidently the man

Ludwig had been in the grove as Steve and Eddie stole up to the radio shack.   Had he seen them?   Or had they made some slight sound which had aroused his suspicions?

"How are you with a gun?" Steve whispered.

"Too good for my own best interests," Eddie replied softly.   "That's why I need Chambert's protection."

Feeling around with his foot Steve located a stone the size of a small eggplant.   He heard the three radiomen beating their way through the grove slowly and systematically.   It looked like a fight.

While he was not afraid of the impending fight, Steve suddenly realized that any sort of noise would bring the whole camp on their heads.

"We mustn't fight," he whispered to Eddie.   "We mustn't fight."

"Yeah?   We can't get away and I'm not giving in without a scrap."

"Wait."   Steve glanced about wildly.   Somehow, he knew, they must escape these men and carry on as though unaware of Chambert's schemes.   He must dodge the fight in order to put Chambert and his men out of action.   He tapped Eddie's shoulder, whispering, "Up the tree.   Climb the tree."

"Huh?"

"Go on.   Up the tree."

"We can handle them."

"We've got to do more than handle them.   We've

got to put the whole outfit behind bars.   Climb!"

Eddie swung himself up through the sweeping branches without another word.   Steve followed him. The boughs bent, but there was no sound of their ascent.   They halted about fifteen feet from the ground and flattened their bodies against the trunk.

Below them, they heard the search draw closer. A moment later one of the three men had pushed aside the branches and was examining the spot they had just left.   Those men weren't overlooking a thing.

Steve and Eddie clung to the trunk while the search went past them. They didn't speak.   Minutes passed.   At last they heard the three men walking back to the radio shack and talking in low tones. Again there was light as all three entered the shack and closed the door.

For a good ten minutes more Steve held to the trunk without moving.   Then he reached up and tapped Eddie's foot.   Cautiously he climbed down the tree.   His hands were sticky with resin.   Eddie dropped to the pine-needle ground beside him. Without a word they set off for the lodge.

When they could see the outlines of the lodge against the sky, Steve stopped.   There was always the possibility that Chambert might go to his room and find it empty, but he had to take that chance. There were questions to be answered.

"When you found that radio shack," he asked softly, "what was going on?"

"I don't know, I don't speak German," Eddie replied. "You heard that dance band? Well, I think it's some sort of code."

"How do you mean?"

"I heard a dance band playing just like we heard when we went back there. And there was a vocal. After the guy on the radio got through singing, they switched it off and I could hear them talking German. Then they went on the air with a phonograph record. There was a vocal in it, but here's the catch —I think it was one of those three guys singing."

"In German?"

"No, he sang in English. It was that old popular song *You're the Top*. Remember?"

"Yes, but I don't get it."

"Neither did I at first, then I remembered that he seemed to put special emphasis on certain words. I think they pass along messages that way. To anybody listening in, it sounds like a bum singer on a bum station trying to sound like Bing Crosby."

"But what sort of messages could they pass along?"

"The movements of convoys and bombers. Listen, Steve, this guy Chambert is the biggest broker of maritime insurance in Canada. That's just one of the strings to his bow."

"Then he'd be likely to get plenty of information

on ship movements," Steve agreed. He thought a moment. "Eddie, I've been a plain, unvarnished fool. I should have suspected Chambert from the first, but I was too sore at Major Sears to use my head."

"Well, what are you going to do?"

"I'm not sure. I'll have to play it as I see it, but I can tell you one thing. Mister Chambert has been brewing plenty of trouble in his little kettle—and the pot has boiled over."

"I'm with you, Steve."

"Swell. What we've got to do, if it's humanly possible, is to turn over the whole crew to the Canadian Government."

"Suppose we can't?"

"Then we've got to wreck as much of this place as we can before they—before they take care of us," Steve finished significantly.

"Got a gun?" Eddie asked.

"No."

"Take this one. I'll get another." Eddie handed Steve his gun which proved to be a Colt .45 automatic. "Sorry I can't spare you an extra clip of cartridges."

"I hope I won't need these," Steve replied. "Now, we'll go on as though everything were just as it had been—and wait for our break."

"Check. Think you can find your way back to your room all right?"

"Sure."

"Then I'll sneak back to my quarters. Oh, say," Eddie paused, "what's the signal that things have gone wrong and to start wrecking?"

"Shots," Steve replied. "If you hear me shooting or I hear you shooting, we'll know they've found out that we're on to their little game. Shots are the signal."

Back in his room, Steve pulled a chair over to the window and stared into the darkness as he tried to work out some scheme to defeat Chambert. He certainly had stuck his head into the lion's mouth.

"Act first and think second, that's Knight every time," he growled at himself. "You go round feeling sorry for yourself and being mad at everybody and what does it get you? A double helping of trouble."

"How many men did Chambert have on his hunting grounds," Steve wondered. "I know about the fifteen pilots, the servants in the lodge, and Chambert, Eddie, and myself. But how many others? Were there more than three Nazi radiomen?"

As dawn came up, he was still struggling with a plan to notify the authorities without giving Chambert or a single one of his men time to escape.

After an ice cold shower, he stuck Eddie's automatic inside his shirt and went down to breakfast. Raoul Chambert was at the table before him and he looked at Steve curiously.

"Steve. You look tired. Did you not sleep well?"

"Uh—I slept all right," Steve replied. On sheer inspiration he added, "But I dreamed all night. I was having a dogfight with Major Sears."

"Ah? Sears, eh?"

"Yes. And I shot him down—the dog."

As Steve started to eat, Chambert hitched his chair closer to the young American flier.

"How would you like to do in reality what you have dreamed last night?"

"Shoot down Sears?" Steve asked, his mouth full of bacon. "I'd love it."

"Good. Of course you must realize it will not be Sears himself that you shoot down, but," Chambert added hurriedly, "it will amount to the same thing."

"When do I start?"

"Tonight. Today coming up by boat are powerful searchlights. These my mechanics will mount on our bombers. Tonight you will fly off with ten bombers and machine-gun the planes leaving from Hatties Field."

Steve nodded his head vigorously and went on chewing. Chambert hitched closer as he continued:

"You see, *mon ami,* tonight, at midnight, my friend arrives and I hope to be able to tell him of our triumph."

"What's his name?" Steve asked idly, stalling for time.

"He has a German name," Chambert explained

carefully, "but he is, like you, an American. His name is von Rein."

As Steve lifted his coffee cup to his lips, he was sure that the sudden trembling of his hand must give away his surprise. Von Rein! Why von Rein had been taken before a Court of Admiralty in Central America because of his submarine activities in which the Devil's Hand had been his base. Steve's adventures with Pedro Hennessey and Venga Savricas, and his previous encounter with von Rein were told in *The Mystery of the Devil's Hand.*

"He has just arrived from Central America where he was in the service of your Government," Chambert said smoothly. "I believe he broke up a ring of Nazi pirates down there."

"Must be a good man," Steve remarked. He hoped his voice didn't sound as funny to Chambert as it sounded to himself. "And he'll be here by midnight?"

"Yes. I am sending Eddie for him." Chambert looked at him closely. "But you, you have not said how you like my plan?"

"Well—I don't like it."

"Eh?" Chambert pushed back his chair and rose, his eyes cold. "Please to explain yourself, Monsieur."

"Now take it easy," Steve drawled. He couldn't stall any longer if von Rein was coming. "First let me tell you what I don't like about it."

"Please do so."

"We want to show your friend—what was his name?"

"His name does not matter. What do *we* want to show him?"

"We want to show him we know how to make a bum out of Sears. Suppose we shoot down a couple of bombers—so what?"

"I do not understand," said Chambert coldly.

"I can see that," Steve replied negligently. It was now or never. If von Rein saw him it would be all over. He had to think of something and think of it fast. He tried to be casual while his mind raced. "No, I can see that you don't understand."

"Please to explain."

"What good does it do to shoot up a couple of bombers?"

"You have, I presume, a better idea?" Chambert asked suspiciously.

"Of course I have," Steve replied confidently. His mind was a blank. "Sit down and listen."

"I do not know that I like your attitude." Chambert leaned across the table and stared at Steve. "Your explanation, Monsieur?"

"What we want to do is wreck Hatties Field, wreck the whole works," Steve said recklessly. "You say shoot down a few ships. I say throw a monkey wrench into the works. Fix it so that not a plane can leave Hatties for two months."

"Ah," Chambert purred. He sat down slowly,

his eyes never leaving Steve's face. "And why do you say we should wreck Hatties Field?"

"Because Sears runs the plane end, that's why. If we're going to give him the business, let's do it right."

"Steve, I have not appreciated you. They tell me the Americans are good haters, but still I have not appreciated you."

"Well, it's about time you did," Steve replied.

"But how do you propose to wreck the field?"

"Why—why bomb it of course."

"Bomb it?"

"Sure." Steve plunged on recklessly. "Listen, the squadron will take off with six bombers and—and three pursuit ships."

"Why not ten bombers?"

"No, we can lay all the eggs we'll need to with six bombers. And we'll need at least three pursuit ships for protection." As he talked, a plan was forming in Steve's mind. He went on, "We'll shove off at midnight. We'll fly around and come in to Hatties Field from the sea."

"And why that?" Chambert asked, but without suspicion in his tone.

"Then it will look as though we might have come from an airplane carrier. We'll bomb the field, fly east again, circle around, and arrive back here. The whole trip should take us about five hours. That is," Steve amended, "five hours for the bombers.

The pursuit ships will have to fly back direct hoping that they are unnoticed in the excitement."

"Excellent, excellent," Chambert cried. He patted Steve on the shoulder. "The pursuit ships arrive, you report. I will turn to my friend and say, 'Monsieur von Rein, my squadron has destroyed Hatties Field!' Imagine his surprise."

"Just imagine it," Steve echoed, his mind busy. Again he had put his head in the lion's mouth. How was he going to get out of this?

"Tell me, do you think the squadron will lose many planes on this mission?"

"I don't think we'll lose any," Steve replied. "It will come as such a complete surprise that the only thing we need fear is a lucky hit by the AA guns. I myself will fly one of the pursuit ships in the event that any fighters take off against us. We must not be trailed back here."

"Ah, no. That would be disastrous."

"It is better," Steve remarked significantly, "if none of our bombers return than if our base is discovered. I will guarantee that no fighter plane follows the pursuit ships."

"Good. Even if we lose a pilot or two, it doesn't matter much." Chambert's smile was oily. "My friend von Rein can supply us with pilots if we but show him your plan is practical."

"I'll do that all right," Steve promised. He rose.

"I'm going out to plan the details with the squadron."

Walking down to the squadron's quarters with the memory of Chambert's oily smile in his mind, Steve fought the problem of what to do next. He had prepared a perfect net—the squadron would be gone, Chambert and von Rein would be in the lodge. But where did he go from there?

How could he get in touch with Sears? How could he warn the men at Hatties Field of the proposed attack? It was hopeless to try luring the squadron away from their announced destination. Captain Smith was too shrewd to be deceived by faked flying directions.

Yes, he had prepared the perfect net—and now he himself was caught in it.

XIV.

Bombs for Friends

ALL morning, while rehearsing the squadron for its raid on Hatties Field, Steve had kept a sharp lookout for Eddie, but Chambert's aerial chauffeur had not put in an appearance. At lunch with Chambert he had voiced the wish that Eddie could come along on the raid as one of the bomber pilots. Chambert had pointed out that Eddie was flying to pick up von Rein. But Chambert had not said where Eddie was at the moment nor where he was likely to be.

While Chambert was taking his usual afternoon siesta, Steve had set off on a casual walk. His objective was to run into Eddie and make it appear as accidental as possible. But he was blocked. As he skirted the flying field, Captain Smith seemed to come from nowhere. The blonde pilot dropped into step with Steve.

"Taking a constitutional?" Smith inquired pleasantly.

Afraid that his nervousness might show, Steve decided on a candid attitude. "Yes." He grinned and went on, "This is my first crack at anything like tonight's raid and I felt myself beginning to tighten up."

"I don't blame you," Smith replied, "you've got the toughest assignment. I'm glad I'm flying a bomber and not one of the fighters."

"Oh, it shouldn't be so bad. All I have to do is cruise around with the other two pursuit ships and keep the R.A.F. fighters off your necks." Steve was keeping his eyes open for Eddie as Smith and he strolled along. He wasn't quite sure how he could shake Smith if he sighted Eddie—he'd have to see how things broke. "I wish I had three more pilots or three more bombardiers."

"It certainly would help," Smith agreed.

"Couldn't we press some of the ground crew into service as bombardiers?" Steve asked.

"No. Mr. Chambert wouldn't like it."

"I know. Here we have fifteen pilots and all we can put into the air is three fighters and six bombers. Including myself, that's three pilots for the fighters and two-men crews for each bomber, except yours, which is to carry a radioman."

"I feel sure that Mr. Chambert would not agree to our using any of the ground crew as a bombardier," Smith repeated.

"I asked him to let me borrow Eddie, his chauffeur, and he turned me down cold."

"You asked for Eddie?" There was surprise in Smith's voice.

"Yes, but no business. It's too bad. Eddie's a good pilot."

"Yes," agreed Smith, but he didn't seem enthusiastic.

Still no sign of Eddie.

Seeing a trail that headed off into the woods in the direction of the radio shack Eddie had shown him the night before, Steve was about to follow it, when he noticed a change in Smith's attitude. The man halted and caught Steve's arm lightly.

"Oh, by the way, Colonel, have you seen my collection?"

"Collection of what?" Steve asked.

"Collection of music boxes. Come, I would like to show it to you."

"Let's see where this trail goes first," Steve suggested innocently.

Smith's hold on his arm tightened slightly. "Let me show you my collection," he urged. "You will find it most interesting."

To have insisted on following the trail might have brought matters to a head. Steve was not prepared for that yet. He yielded to Smith's urging and they turned and started off for the squadron's quarters.

"A collection of music boxes," Steve mused. "I never heard of a man collecting music boxes before."

"In my country many men collect them," Smith replied stiffly.

"Yeah? What is your country?" Steve asked innocently.

"Switzerland. I am Swiss. I was born in Kreuzlingen, which is on the shores of Lake Constance. That is the canton of Thurgau." Smith recited the information as though he had memorized it and not as though it was the result of childhood memories.

"How long have you been over here?" Steve asked casually.

Again Smith seemed to recite. "I came to this country as a child of four with my father. We moved to Winnipeg, which is in the province of Manitoba, where my father secured work as a watch repairman."

"I've been to Winnipeg," Steve remarked. "My father was related to Alfred Andrews who was Mayor of Winnipeg once."

"You have been to Winnipeg?" Smith asked, and then went on without a break, "It is a lovely city, but I lived there but two years and then my father moved to Vancouver, British Columbia."

"I've never been to Vancouver," Steve remarked.

"Ah. It was there I lived until I came to work for Mr. Chambert."

"Oh yeah?" Steve thought to himself. "I wonder what you'd have said if I'd said I knew Vancouver well? I bet you'd have moved to Medicine Hat or Fort William or up to Hudson's Bay. Your English is pretty good, Steve admitted, but I don't think you learned it in Canada, I don't believe you were born in Switzerland, and I'd bet plenty your name isn't Smith. But it might be Schmidt."

They entered the squadron's quarters and Smith showed Steve his collection of music boxes. In all, he had twenty-six of them and they ranged in size from one that was shaped like an egg and as small, to one that was almost as large as a football.

Throughout his inspection, Steve managed to ask questions at the right time but his mind was busy with another problem. At midnight the squadron took off for Hatties Field. The six bombers would carry two tons of bombs each—and they were real bombs. Somehow, Steve must prevent those bombs from being dropped, and at the same time, he must get to Major Sears and tell him about Chambert. How could he do it? At the first sight of his deserting the squadron, the whole crew might jettison their bombs and head back to warn Chambert. Or they might radio him of Steve's desertion. Or they— there were a thousand possibilities.

Six bombers and two fighters beside himself. Six bombers—twelve tons of bombs. Twelve tons of incendiary bombs that would turn the unsuspecting field into a roaring inferno. And it had seemed like such a smart idea when he had suggested it to Chambert that morning. It had been the perfect plan.

That had been this morning. This was now. If

he could only find Eddie, he might arrange it so that the chauffeur could warn the authorities when he went to pick up von Rein. But, so far as he knew, Eddie didn't even have any knowledge of the mission on which the squadron would set out shortly before he returned with von Rein. Eddie didn't know and there seemed to be slight hope of Steve getting in touch with him.

Maybe this was the spot to start shooting. Steve glanced about the living room of the squadron's lodge. Three of his pilots were playing cards in the corner. He could get out Eddie's automatic that nestled against his ribs inside his shirt and get Smith and the card players before they knew what hit them. That left eleven pilots—and three shots.

All right, he'd set fire to the lodge. In the excitement he'd be able to get to Chambert before——

"My Colonel," Smith was saying, "my collection bores you. A thousand pardons."

"Not at all, not at all," Steve mumbled. He rose. "I was just running over our plans for tonight in my mind."

"They will be successful and much of that success we owe to you." Smith stood up, clicking his heels as he saluted. "Short as the time has been, you have done wonders with the squadron."

"Thank you, Captain." Steve returned the salute. "I'll see you later."

As he had started back to the main lodge, he had been sure that eyes were watching his departure from the squadron's lodge. But there had been no attempt to follow him.

His hopes of running into Eddie on the way back had proved empty. Back in his room, Steve paced the floor. It was broad daylight and there was absolutely no chance of his slipping out unobserved to search for Eddie.

There was no way out. And there was no use kidding himself—again he had gotten himself into a mess. And there was no hope of calling on Eddie to get him out of it. He'd simply have to rely on himself.

Six bombers would circle low over Hatties Field and drop incendiaries at their leisure. How could he stop them?

When Steve showed up at dinner he was hollow-eyed. Chambert studied him attentively with raised eyebrows. He smiled as he asked, "Come, my friend, surely you did not once more dogfight with Major Sears?"

"No," Steve said. Candor had disarmed Smith, he'd try it on Chambert. "I've been thinking about tonight. I hate to think of the men who may get hurt, but—but it's got to be."

Chambert watched him and did not reply.

"Are you sure," Steve leaned across the table, "are you sure they'll break Sears after our raid?"

"I am positive."

"Don't you—isn't there a chance that he might have enough pull to shift the blame to someone else?"

"No," Chambert began but checked himself. "My dear Steve, I must tell you the truth—there is always that chance. He has much influence."

Steve slapped the table. "Then we can't afford to lose any bombers."

"No? And why not?"

"If they don't break Sears after this raid, we've got to go on raiding them until they do break him."

"Excellent! A splendid idea!" Chambert watched him closely as he asked, "But will not many innocent men suffer for Sears' sins?"

"That can't be helped," Steve declared stubbornly. "Besides, most of our damage will be done to the hangars housing the bombers, the machine shops, and the field itself."

"How soon do you think they will be able perhaps to repair the damage you do?"

"Who can answer that for sure?" Steve replied. Then his tone became aggressive and his hard eyes met Chambert's. "But I'll bet you one thing—I'll bet not a plane leaves Hatties for two weeks after we get through."

Turning his head down so Steve might not see the gleam of satisfaction in his eyes, Chambert murmured, "And that could have been avoided if they had not murdered your friends."

Steve busied himself with his dinner. The execution of Hugh Gracey and Corky Merlin had been murder, pure murder. But he wasn't going to help professional murderers to win just because Sears and the Navy people had made a tragic blunder.

But how was he going to stop it?

Again the question that had plagued him all afternoon. Dinner ended and the need for keeping up a conversation with Chambert gave him no time to continue the hunt for a solution. Any hope Steve entertained of going to his room after dinner and working on his problem was defeated by his host.

"Come, Colonel," Chambert remarked as they rose from the table, "take me into your confidence now. Show me how you will attack the British at Hatties Field."

There was nothing else he could do. Chambert sent a servant for the maps Steve had worked on and the young flier laid them out on the table. He used a pencil as a pointer.

"We leave at one minute past midnight and fly north-northeast until we have rounded Cape Bald —here." He pointed to the northern tip of Newfoundland. "We fly at 15,000 feet minimum. Rounding Cape Bald, we curve to the east and then southeast keeping a good fifty miles off the Newfoundland coast. In event of separation, we met at

50 degrees longitude, 45 degrees latitude at exactly three-thirty."

"But does that not mean one must take bearings and, how do you say, shoot the sun or is it the moon?"

"Frankly," Steve explained, "I'm going to shepherd the planes like a collie. Smith is competent to be at the meeting place at the appointed time and it will be my job to see that all other planes follow him."

"But all these directions and this talk of longitude and latitude," Chambert asked.

Steve glanced about. "That's merely to give the men a greater feeling of confidence. If they are able to take bearings, we'll be there."

"Ah, it is then merely for their morale?"

"Exactly. We'll come in to Hatties Field from the east. The people there will have no way of telling whether we came from a plane carrier, Iceland, Norway, or what. The bombers will drop down to unload their bombs while the fighters remain at 15,-000 feet."

"But why do the fighters remain so high?"

"Our presence would be a tip-off that we hadn't made a long trip. Also," Steve added, "we'll be in better position to intercept any attack that may be made by night fighters."

"Excellent reasoning, Colonel. Excellent."

"As soon as our mission is completed, the bombers turn and climb toward the east. Upon meeting us, we swing back at maximum altitude and return to our bases. The fighters wait only long enough to be sure there is no pursuit and then return here. We should arrive a good thirty minutes before the bombers."

"I cannot tell you how much I admire your strategy," Chambert said. He sounded sincere and Steve writhed inwardly. He was finding it increasingly difficult to look at Chambert, for fear of revealing his true feelings for the man. "I am sure your mission will meet with success and now, Monsieur, I salute you."

"Thank you. I hope your friend Mr. von Rein approves."

"Von Rein is sure to approve," Chambert exclaimed. "Especially since we shall present him with *un fait accompli.*"

"That means something already accomplished, doesn't it?"

"But truly. Von Rein is somewhat doubtful of one's ability as a strategist. This will prove enlightening."

"That was something to remember," Steve thought. Evidently Chambert and von Rein had worked together before and evidently the Gestapo agent was not a complete admirer of Chambert's prowess. The Frenchman glanced at his watch and whistled.

"*Alors.* The time flies. I must send Eddie to his

rendezvous with my guest." He rose and bowed. "You will excuse me?"

Steve nodded dully. As Chambert left the room, Steve had a wild impulse to start firing. That would send Eddie into action and they would have to take their chances on nabbing Chambert and fighting their way out—he stopped himself. That was sheer insanity.

Three hours remained before the take-off. He had three hours in which to find a way out of the trap he had laid for Chambert, which had, in turn, trapped Steve himself. Three hours!

XV.

The Raid

IT WAS midnight.

Chambert, Steve, Captain Smith and the fourteen other pilots of the squadron gathered in the Number One bomber hangar. Steve faced his men.

"You all have your orders, you know exactly what to do. Are there any questions?"

There were no questions.

"Very well. Bombers take off behind Captain Smith. The three pursuit ships will take off in thirty minutes."

"But suppose Monsieur von Rein arrives as you are taking off?" Chambert demanded.

"Then von Rein must wait. Contrary to the usual flying field procedure, we will have the right of way."

"As you wish, Colonel," Chambert replied curtly.

It was a break that von Rein hadn't arrived, Steve thought. It gave him an extra half hour—and he might be able to stretch it out a bit longer—when an extra half hour's fuel meant everything.

"All right, Captain Smith. Take off with your men."

Smith, his bombardier, and radioman clambered into their plane. The two-man crew of the second bomber went to their ship. The hoists growled as the underground door opened. The motors roared.

Steve and Chambert rode up to the surface with Smith's bomber. There was a brief moment and then the big ship hurtled off down the dark field. Before it had traveled twenty-five yards the lights went on. It soared up and was lost for a moment against the darkness of the forest that hemmed them in, and then appeared as the moonlight glinted on its sleek body. The field lights went off.

A moment later the second bomber roared down the field after Smith. Again the sudden glare of field lights, again the plane's disappearance against the dark backdrop of black fir, and again its reappearance as it was outlined against the sky and the glint of the moon.

One after another the six bombers took off, their bomb racks loaded with destruction. Steve's knees felt weak as he watched them go. This was his doing and as yet he had found no way out. As a matter of fact, he had not had a moment to himself.

Now the bombers were gone and the air no longer echoed to their heavy roar. With Chambert at his side and the two other fighter pilots behind him, Steve led the way to one of the secret hangars that housed the fighters. The ground crew trotted ahead of them.

He looked at his watch as he went below ground. It seemed almost impossible, but twenty-five minutes had elapsed since Captain Smith took off. On the pretext of examining the three pursuit ships, Steve managed to use up fifteen minutes.

"Hurry, my Colonel, hurry," Chambert was urging. His teeth shone in the half light of the hangar. "They will drop their calling cards on Hatties Field without you."

"I doubt it," Steve replied. There was nothing for it. He said, "See you soon," and climbed into the cockpit of his plane.

The elevator arrangement carried them to the surface and his plane roared to life. For a second Steve watched his gauges—everything was percolating. He waved his hand.

As the ground crew yanked the blocks from under his wheels, the Messerschmitt seemed to hurl itself forward. The next instant Steve was blinded by dazzling light from all sides. His eyes grew accustomed to it and he saw the red light—he eased back on the stick. He was up to the green light—he eased back a trifle more. The vibration stopped and he knew he was in the air.

Climbing sharply, he glanced back to watch the two other planes take off. They followed him without a hitch. With them behind him, Steve climbed through a cloudless sky and set off at a right angle to intercept the bombers after they had swung around past Cape Bald.

And now for a plan.

That was easy enough to say, but Steve found it impossible to put into action. No plan came. He buzzed along at 18,000 feet with the two other fighters behind him. Flying was purely automatic in this cloudless, windless sky.

But while no plan presented itself, Steve was conscious of a slowly mounting rage. Those six bombers were bent on destroying an unsuspecting flying field. They were bent on sowing death among men who had been his friends and companions.

Major Jeff Sears and the men who had condemned Hugh Gracey and Corky to death might have blundered in what they considered the meting out of justice, but they had tried to be fair. It was he, Steve, who had lost his head, turned sulky, and behaved like a perfect young fool.

Of one thing Steve was morally certain—Sears never would drop from the friendly sky to rain death on unsuspecting people below. And something else came back to him. He remembered now how anxious the squadron had been to start on its mission. Every one of those fifteen men was itching to see not merely the camp destroyed, but the destruction of the men in Hatties Field.

And Steve could think of no way to stop it.

Away below he saw the six bombers flying in echelon. In the moonlight, they seemed suspended in air. It was a peaceful sight, but Steve knew they were murderers. Six bombers below him and two fighters behind.

His earphones crackled and a voice said, "Calling, Colonel Knight. To Colonel Knight. Captain Smith's compliments, sir. We meet on schedule."

"Proceed according to orders," Steve answered, his lips stiff.

He glanced at his watch. In exactly twelve minutes they would heel about and start east. Nineteen minutes later the bombers would peel off and dive on Hatties Field, unloading death as they went. Steve looked down and marked Captain Smith's plane. Smith had the only plane equipped to radio Chambert's lodge if necessary. The chances were that some sort of secret signals had been arranged and that at this moment Chambert was aware of their progress.

Steve could picture Chambert sitting before the fire being handed regular bulletins sent out from Smith's plane. Chambert must be licking his lips in anticipation.

Below him, the bomber formation heeled over and headed due east—and Steve knew what he must do. Smith was first. He hated to attack without warning, but he must get Smith before Chambert could be warned.

After Smith, he must take his chance with the other seven planes. He must shoot them out of the sky if he could. If they got him, he must pray that his attack disorganized the raid sufficiently to warn the men in Hatties Field or delay the bombing attack.

Pulling up his nose, Steve peeled off and dove down at Smith's plane in a twisting, all-out dive. The plane showed up clearing in the center of his sights. He waited. Smith's plane grew larger and larger.

Steve pressed the trigger and felt his plane vibrate wildly as he poured four hundred shots per second into the bomber on his sights. It took only a second or two. The bomber dipped suddenly. Steve whipped around to face the next bombers glancing over his shoulder as he did so.

Smoke poured blackly from the bomber as it plunged downward. A moment later a black shape detached itself and went floating out into space in an arc. Another black shape followed. Then a parachute fluttered open from the first black dot.

Stunned at what had happened, the other five bombers were still flying in perfect formation. Steve caught one on the right in his sights and fired. Again his plane vibrated to the stream of fire that poured from his wings. Again the black smoke followed the bomber's downward plunge.

But now the surprise was over. As Steve turned

to come up under the third bomber, the air around him steamed with tracer bullets. He twisted sideways in a quick barrel roll that put the plane he was attacking between him and the machine gunners in the other bombers.

The strategy outmaneuvered the men at the machine guns, but it also gave his quarry a chance to escape. Steve did a snap roll and was after him. His quarry was climbing. Steve came up under and behind him. As he jockeyed into position for a burst at the bomber's belly, the bombardier raced back to the tail turret and fought to line up his machine guns on Steve's plane.

Tracer bullets were drawing pencils of light around his right wing. Steve did a sudden vertical reverse and found a bomber almost on top of him. He fired a wild burst and did a split S and went after his former quarry. He had no idea what had happened to the plane on his tail, but for a moment he was free of attack.

"Take your time," he said aloud. "Take your time. Stick with one until you get him."

His former quarry was dead ahead and a little below him. Steve zoomed.

But again the air about him smoked with tracer bullets. This time they came from several different angles. He stuck to his quarry. Either the pilot below was unaware of his danger or he had gone into a complete mental blank. Steve was diving straight for his tail and the bomber made no attempt to dodge out of range.

That was fine. But at the same time at least three planes were playing the identical game with Steve as their target. They were wasting ammunition at this particular second, but sooner or later—it wasn't sensible to give three planes a perfect shot at him.

Using his momentum, Steve whipped into an Immelmann. As he rolled over, he saw that two bombers and one fighter had been on his tail. He came in a 45-degree bank and opened his guns on the tangle below him.

Panic-stricken by the loss of his quarry and the sudden fire from above, the fighter whirled about wildly. The pilot froze to the trigger and Steve could see the pattern of his tracer bullets cutting along the side of the bomber on the fighter's right. The bomber did a roll almost lazily, started upward, stalled, and hurtled down in a twisting dive.

Before the fighter could recover, Steve pounced on him. He had the fighter on his sights and opened up. Someone was rapping on the side of his ship, but Steve kept his sights on the fighter and his finger on the trigger.

He saw his tracer bullets streaking into the fighter, but still the plane seemed unharmed. The rapping continued on his door. Ridiculously, Steve yelled, "Come in."

It was surprising that the rapping continued. It

was miraculous that the plane below him was un-harmed by his own burst of—suddenly the fighter burst in mid-air. Steve dove.

Now the rapping had stopped. He glanced over and found that machine gun bullets had chewed away a section of the fuselage just behind his seat. As he pulled the plane up into a loop with quarter roll recovery, Steve was relieved to find that the con-trols seemed unharmed by the bullets which had passed completely through his plane.

One fighter—three bombers. Steve banked about to see what was left. There should be three other bombers and one fighter still to account for.

As he came about, he ran almost head on into a withering fire. He dove and veered around to the left as he went. The maneuver shook two of his attackers, but one of them stuck with him. Steve went into a vertical bank with the bomber right be-hind him.

But his superior speed and greater maneuverabil-ity gave Steve the edge. He rolled out of his bank but instead of trying for the bomber on his tail, he streaked head on for the other two bombers.

Roaring down at them at right angles to their line of flight, he opened up with his gun deliberately al-though he was still out of range. The bombers looked ghostly in the bright moonlight. The next moment, tracer bullets were weaving a spider web around his tail assembly. The bomber had re-turned to the fight.

His ship full-out, Steve headed for the two bombers. Suddenly they became aware of his approach. They separated and scattered wildly, firing as they went. Steve knifed between them and banked around in a flat climb.

The confusion caused by the scattering bombers had shaken the one on his tail. Steve climbed slightly with his throttle wide. He glanced back to see what the situation was behind him. The three bombers were whipping about to set out after him, but he had a lead of a good 300 feet altitude on them.

That, plus their slower rate of climb, gave him a definite edge for perhaps the first time since Steve had dropped down on Smith's back. He continued his circling climb, trying to divine what their next move would be. To attack at this point, straight into the turret guns of those three bombers, would be to ask for trouble.

Gaining altitude steadily, Steve circled around watching the three planes below. They had formed a wedge and were flying about as though uncertain what to do next. Abruptly, they banked and headed off in a group. Steve glanced at his compass. They were headed for Hatties Field.

So that was it. They were going to lay their eggs in spite of him. Steve heeled over and set out in pursuit. He overhauled the flying wedge below him rapidly.

The bombers passed out of sight below him. Now was the time, he had to take his chances with the three guns in the turret of each plane below him. Steve pulled up his nose to peel off for his dive. As he turned over on his back, twisting over and down, the third fighter materialized out of the moonlight above him, his wing guns blazing.

Steve could see the spit of fire from the wing guns. Blindly, he fired a burst, hoping he might get in a lucky shot. And in a flash, he realized the trap into which he had fallen so neatly.

It took only a second to see what had happened. While he had been gaining altitude, the remaining fighter had done the same thing. So far it had stayed out of the fight waiting for an opening. Well, Steve had given it to him.

He had allowed the bombers to decoy him into watching them to the exclusion of everything else. And while he had watched the bombers, the fighter had stalked him at leisure.

He whirled downward in a spinning dive. But he was outlined against the moonlit water and the fighter clung to him tenaciously, its wing guns hammering him unmercifully. His hands on the controls were sensitive to every bullet that struck the plane, and those bullets were bouncing along his left wing working nearer and nearer to the fuselage.

He spun about, but the fighter above him spun with him. And for a good ten seconds of every revolution, the bullets would find his wing. He straightened out and pointed the nose down and opened the throttle.

Now he'd find out. He'd dive this plane until the wings fell off. Maybe that guy on his tail wouldn't dare risk it. Maybe he'd pull out of his dive.

But he didn't!

Steve was aware of sudden panic. This guy in the fighter was going to get him, get him sure. He glanced out at his left wing. He could almost touch the holes the fighter's guns were punching out on the wing metal. He pushed the nose down. He was dropping almost vertically. And with the motor full-out.

And then he saw the bombers just below him. They had scattered and were twisting to get out of the path of the two plunging planes. And Steve saw an escape. It came in a flash.

As he passed the bombers, he slewed the plane around. The wings might sheer off, the strain might crack the fuselage in two, but it was the only chance. He yanked up the nose and twisted the plane around.

The right wing responded, but the left wing dragged. It was as though the plane had been tossed sideways, wing over wing, by a giant hand. He rolled around and came up. By main force, he dragged the nose around.

Just above him and to the left was one of the bombers. He got it on his sights and fired. The plane disintegrated before his eyes. But where had the fighter gone? He looked around.

Now he was even with another bomber and the

man in the turret was turning the guns on him. Steve fired. His burst sliced off the tail and the plane fell out of control.

Now the score was five bombers—one fighter.

He looked around. Below him he saw white mushrooms floating slowly down to the water below. It would be plenty cold in that water, but the men would not drown, they all had kapok jackets.

But where was the fighter? And the other bomber?

Suddenly Steve realized why he couldn't see the bomber and the fighter—there was land ahead. The dark bodies of the planes were lost against the dark mass of land. And land meant Hatties Field.

Ahead and to the left there was a sudden burst of fire. The bomber had jettisoned its bomb load and the deadly missiles were exploding in the water. But where was the fighter and where was the camp?

As though in answer, lights glared on below him and outlined the field. Steve's plane was limping. He was in no position to set out after the remaining planes of the squadron.

Now to get down and start Sears and his men out for Chambert's hunting grounds.

XVI.

Man Hunt

PLANES were taking off on the field below him, their exhausts belching orange flame in the cold white light of the floodlights. They were fighters and they took off cross wind. Three came up together, then three more, then another three.

Bombers trundled out into the floodlights' glare, but made no move to take off. Steve was grateful that he hadn't been greeted with a burst of flak from the anti-aircraft guns. The bombers below seemed to be waiting for him to land.

One of the trio of fighters that had taken off circled Steve's limping plane briefly before streaking off to the east. "Why hadn't the fighters attacked him," Steve wondered? There was no mistaking the lines of his plane, its square wing tips. The average twelve-year-old would recognize it as a 'Schmitt.

"Be thankful they didn't hop you," he said aloud.

Yes, he was hardly in any shape for aerobatics. The left wing was dragging badly. He came into the field slowly and very flat. Steve fought to lift that crippled left wing. He pushed the lever to put down his retractable landing gear.

Still fighting the drag in his left wing, Steve settled closer and closer to the ground. Suddenly the floodlights on the left side of the field begin to jiggle up and down. He shook his head to clear it. The lights continued to jiggle.

Steve glanced at them. No, it wasn't imagination —those lights were being moved rapidly up and down. He saw a group of men running out on the field. They seemed to be yelling at him, but he was unable to hear them. They were trying to signal him, to tell him something—but what?

On a hunch, he snapped off the ignition. He was not a moment too soon. Abruptly the plane touched ground. The next moment it slewed around and went tumbling wing over wing. Steve felt himself go over twice. . . .

From a long way off someone said, "Here he comes."

"He'll be coming 'round the mountain when he comes," Steve replied drowsily. Something was awfully funny, he laughed and murmured, "Pin-wheel Knight, good old Pin-wheel Knight."

"Give him another shot of ammonia," a voice urged.

Steve was aware of a peculiar odor and then his mouth was full of water, only it didn't taste like water. He swallowed and tried to remember what had been so funny. "Good old Pin-wheel———"

"It's all right, boy, it's all right," said a familiar voice.

"Hi say, the chap's balmy," another familiar voice remarked.

Pushing aside things that seemed to clutch at him, Steve pulled himself through a fog. He forced his eyes to focus on the white blur that surrounded him. Slowly the blur dissolved into faces, white faces peering down at him.

"Are you all right now, old man?" asked a man squatting on his heels beside him.

Steve looked at him curiously and suddenly his head swam. Someone pushed the kneeling man aside and growled, "You infernal idiot!" Steve tried to orient himself. That man who had squatted beside him, that man had looked like Hugh Gracey. What was this? Had he gotten the Big One?

"It's all right, Steve. You're all right. You're in Hatties Field. Open your eyes, boy, this is Sears talking. Everything's——"

"Sears!" Steve forced his eyes open again. It wasn't Hugh Gracey, but Major Sears who knelt beside him. "We've got to get them before they can warn Chambert and von Rein." Words tumbled from him and he tried to get up.

"That's the boy," Sears cried. "I knew you'd come through. Now take it easy—what have we got to do?"

"Chambert. He's got a secret flying field. Von Rein's visiting him. We've got to get the bomber and fighter before they can warn him."

"Warm up those planes," Sears shouted over his shoulder. He asked Steve, "Can you give us directions?"

"I'll show you where they are."

"I'm afraid not, Steve, you see—" Sears stopped and looked over his shoulder. He asked, "How about it, Doctor?"

"He's shaken up pretty thoroughly and may be suffering from shock," replied one of the white faces that hemmed Steve in, "but there's no concussion, no broken bones."

"I've got to go," Steve declared hotly. "They've got hidden hangars, hidden radio stations. You'll never find them if I'm not along."

"All right, all right," Sears laughed. "I've been waiting for you to turn up and this is your show. Along you come."

Major Jeff Sears jumped up and barked out orders. Two men helped Steve to rise, they placed his arms over their shoulders and led him to a big transport that stood near by, its four propellers turning lazily. As they went to it, nine bombers took off, three at a time. Steve saw that there were three other bombers in line behind the one to which he was being led.

He was helped up the ladder to the cabin and the

door slammed and locked behind him. There were other men in the cabin, but Steve recognized only Sears in the dim light. He sat down beside Sears.

A moment later the big ship went bumping off across the field. And then it was in the air and speeding west. Sears turned to him and patted his knee as he asked:

"How about some directions, Steve?"

"Head for Bonne Bay on the east coast of New-foundland. Do you know it?"

Sears conferred with the junior officer who bent over him. The officer went into the control cabin.

"All right, boy, we're heading for Bonne Bay. Now take a nap. As soon as we're there I'll wake you up."

Steve closed his eyes gratefully. The minute he did so his head began to do tricks and he opened his eyes again. The spinning stopped. He felt as though he had been tossed around by a giant egg beater. And then he remembered—"Pin-wheel Knight, the only gyrating pilot in the world, step right up, ladies and gentlemen, and see the great Pin-wheel Knight in his special somersault."

That had seemed awfully funny a few seconds ago, but not any more. That business of thinking he'd seen Hugh Gracey—that hadn't been so funny, even at the time. Sears saw that Steve was awake. He handed him a thermos flask and unscrewed the cap.

"Try a cup of coffee, Steve. It'll warm you up."

"Thanks." Steve hated to accept anything from Sears, but the coffee did help. As he worked on a second cup, he asked Sears stiffly, "How come your anti-aircraft didn't open up on me?"

"We saw part of your dogfight," Sears explained. "At first it didn't seem to make much sense—one Schmitt scraping with three Stukas and another Schmitt. But I'd been expecting something like this."

"You'd been expecting it?" Steve asked incredulously.

"Yes, you see—how do you feel?"

"Fine."

"Really? You're not just being a good sport, you really feel all right?"

"Yes."

"Can you stand a bit of a shock?"

"Why—sure."

"All right. I think it will be a pleasant one." Sears snapped on a cabin light and said over his shoulder, "Come on, you two. You can talk to him now."

Steve turned. Two men shuffled up the aisle. Their faces were hidden because they were bent over to avoid the low ceiling of the military plane. And then Steve saw. The leading man held out his hand —Hugh Gracey, it had been Hugh Gracey! And right behind him came Corky Merlin.

Though he tried for words, none came and Steve

could only stare. He hardly heard what Gracey and Corky were trying to say. They pumped his hand and slapped him on the shoulder. Still Steve could only stare.

"I don't get it," he stammered, turning to Sears. "I don't get it."

"It's a long story and I'll try to make it brief," Sears said. "I hated my part in this show, Steve, but Norm Bennett assured me you could take it, so———." He shrugged. "Duty is duty, you know."

"But you told me they'd been shot, you said———."

"I know. That was part of the plan. Steve, we used you just about the same way they use a ram to hunt tigers. Corky is an old Intelligence Service man and Hugh did Intelligence work before he got into the flying end of this war.

"It was really Bennett's idea. He suggested that you and two men I could trust be sent off in a bomber. Gracey was to mess up the navigation so that you would be forced down. Then your friend Helmuth stepped into the picture and shot you down. That wasn't according to plan, nor was your attack on Captain Hansler's vessel, your capture, and subsequent escape.

"However, once you had turned Captain Hansler over to our Navy people, we were able to pick up the thread of our plan where it had been broken. So, as you'll recall, you were arrested, brought back, and tried. It was a very unfair trial because it had to be.

Then, just as Commander Bennett prophesied, you set off to get Hugh and Corky a fair trial."

The copilot spilled into the cabin and saluted Sears.

"Sorry to interrupt, sir, but I just got signal A-26 from our fighters."

"Good, good. Is there any sign of the bomber?"

"None, sir." The officer saluted and returned to the control cabin.

"Our fighters intercepted Chambert's fighter and shot him down. There is no sign of the bomber."

"That's one less chance of Chambert being warned," Steve observed. "But what about your bombers? Where are they bound?"

"By now they have been told to rendezvous at Bonne Bay. Meanwhile they are dragging the sky for that enemy bomber."

"He'll never get away from them," Hugh Gracey said and pointed to the window. "In twenty minutes it'll be light."

"Let me go on with my story, we haven't much time," Sears said. "Norm Bennett said that you were very loyal to your friends and we did everything we could to make you sore at us and convince you that you and Hugh and Corky had been given a raw deal. Well, it worked out pretty well. Chambert got in touch with you—though he was the last man we suspected. Someone had been giving away convoy information for some time, but no one dreamed

Chambert was the traitor. You were sore at us, but unfortunately, you weren't quite sore enough.

"That's why I dropped in and told you that Hugh and Corky had been executed. We had an Intelligence man acting as clerk in your hotel and when he tipped me off that you planned to leave for Ottawa, I hurried right over. I hated to say that Gracey and Merlin had been executed, but it was the straw that broke you down. The next thing we knew, you had vanished. That meant our plan was working, but we were worried because we had no idea where you might be."

"You certainly had us worried," Corky Merlin said without a trace of the cockney accent he had used previously. "Sears kept saying he had sent you to your death."

"Oh, come now. I wasn't that dramatic," Sears objected. "But we were worried. In fact, I got in touch with Commander Bennett and asked him what to do. He told me to stick tight, that the first thing I knew you'd turn up with Chambert in your hip pocket.

"Well, I wasn't quite that optimistic, but I worked out a flight of nine fighters, nine medium bombers, and these four transports so that we'd be prepared for whatever happened. That's another reason our guns didn't fire on you. But, tell me, how did you happen to be in a Schmitt?"

Briefly Steve told of what had happened and how

he had thrown in his lot with Chambert. They gasped when he told them that he had come, as Chambert believed, to bomb Hatties Field.

"So we have to deal with Monsieur Raoul Haye Chambert, eh?" Sears asked as Steve finished. "We should have suspected him sooner, but we didn't. The man has always been a Nazi in his heart."

"From what Steve says," Hugh Gracey put in, "it may have been Chambert who relayed convoy movements to Captain Hansler and the submarines. This flying business of his sounds like a more recent addition."

"I think it is," Steve said. "Maybe he wanted to play a bigger part in the operations. Hansler's capture gave him an excuse to go to town. Besides, if his plan had worked, he'd have done ten times the damage Helmuth and Hansler did—and therefore he could have demanded ten times the reward."

"That sounds reasonable," Sears agreed, "he may have had dreams of being the Canadian fuehrer."

"Bonne Bay," called the copilot sticking his head into the cabin.

"Have you sighted our bombers?" Sears asked.

"Yes. The fighters have all turned back."

"Very good. Well, Steve, it's up to you from here on."

"All right. Can I take the controls?"

"Of course." Sears told the copilot, "Inform Lieutenant Buckley that Mr. Knight will take over and radio the rest of the flight to follow us."

Steve went into the control cabin and slipped into the copilot's seat. Lieutenant Buckley grinned at him and took his hands off the wheel. Steve felt the big ship come to life under his hands. He checked the altitude and headed due west.

Standing at his elbow, Sears said, "I've got eighty men in the four transports, each one armed with a submachine gun. My nine bombers have enough explosives to blow half of Quebec off the map. This is your show, Steve, how shall we use them?"

"I'd like to get von Rein if possible," Steve explained. "How does this hit you? Have the bombers stay aloft to catch anything that tries to escape by land or water. Meanwhile, we'll set the transports down on Chambert's field and round up everyone there."

"Has he any anti-aircraft guns?"

"I don't believe so, we'll just have to take that chance."

"Right. How soon should we be there?"

"Fifteen minutes or less."

"I'll see that your orders get off immediately," Sears promised.

It was growing light below. Now Steve was able to pick out landmarks on the coast he had noticed during his training maneuvers with Chambert's squadron. If they were successful in catching von Rein in their net, it would be a great day's work. Sears came and bent over his shoulder again.

"All ready, Steve, whenever you are."

"And I'm ready now. See that pine grove down there in the middle of that big meadow?"

"Yes. Too bad it's there—the meadow looks like a marvelous landing field."

"It is. And you'll find that the pine grove is composed of trees that don't stand two feet high."

"A nice bit of landscape gardening," commented Sears dryly.

"Here we go," Steve warned. "Hold your hats."

He went down at a sharp angle. At about 800 feet he did a wing slip, and then dropped into the field. As he taxied the plane toward Chambert's lodge to give the other transports plenty of landing room, he saw puffs of smoke coming from a clump of bushes.

Braking to a stop, Steve whirled in his seat. But he had no chance to leave the plane. Sears, Hugh Gracey, Corky Merlin and ten soldiers with sub-machine guns were pouring out, effectively blocking the plane's cabin doors.

"Here," yelled the pilot holding out a pistol to Steve.

"Thanks, I've got one." Steve ripped open his shirt and pulled out the automatic Eddie had given him.

"Hurry, hurry," Lieutenant Buckley urged the men who were clambering out.

At last Steve had a chance. He jumped to the ground. A detachment of twenty men fanned out and was surrounding the lodge. Two lieutenants and four sergeants stood by Sears waiting impatiently for orders.

"Where do they go, Steve?" Sears called.

"See that grove over there?" Steve asked, pointing as he ran to join them. "You better surround it. The radio shack is in the middle of it."

"That's your job, Brown," Sears snapped.

"Very good, sir." Lieutenant Brown grinned as he saluted. "Detail, attention! Open order——"

"How about the hangars?" Sears asked.

"They're all over. Let's not worry about them until later. The machine shops and ground crew quarters are camouflaged by that knoll over there," Steve said, but Sears interrupted him:

"Lieutenant Crandall. Take your detail and clean up that knoll."

"Yes, sir."

"Hey, Steve!" Hugh Gracey called.

Steve wheeled at the call. He followed Gracey's pointing arm. A man rose from a clump of trees and was tottering toward them. It was Eddie. He held a pistol in each hand and was bleeding from a head wound.

As he came toward them there was a sudden burst

of machine gun fire from an upstairs window of the house. Eddie twisted as he pitched forward. A second rattle of machine gun fire drowned out the first. Turning, Steve saw that two of the soldiers advancing on the house had opened fire on the window, silencing the gun that had cut down Eddie.

Steve and Hugh Gracey ran to the fallen man and carried him to the shelter of the plane.

"Thought you'd never come," Eddie murmured weakly. "Von Rein's gone."

"He's gone?" Steve gasped.

"Yes. I was—watching the house. Von Rein was watching sky with field glasses. Spotted you and beat it."

"Couldn't you stop him?"

"That's how I got shot in the head. Chambert heard the shooting, but I fired at him and he went back to the house."

"Then we've got him," Steve exulted.

"I should say we have," Corky Merlin agreed. "Look at that window."

A white pillowcase was being waved from an upstairs window. Steve let out a whoop and turned back to Eddie.

"Where did von Rein go?"

"He headed for the coast."

"Then we've got him," Steve cried. "The bombers will spot him the minute he steps into a boat and he can't get far on foot."

"Here come your radiomen," Sears called out to Steve.

"Nice work, Eddie. We'll patch you up." He watched two soldiers start to give the chauffeur first aid and then joined Sears.

Gunfire broke out from the direction of the knoll, but it ended almost as quickly as it began. The soldiers were closing in. Steve glanced at the lodge just in time to see Lieutenant Brown and two men emerge driving Chambert and his household servants before them.

"And this looks like the end of Mister Chambert," Sears remarked. "Let's go and meet the gentleman, Steve."

"I wish we'd gotten von Rein, but Eddie says he escaped."

"We'll get him," Sears promised confidently.

"Yes, that's what I thought at first, but now—well, I'm not so sure. That man has a charmed life." Steve looked over at the lodge. "Wait a second, Major. Why should we go to Chambert? Let's wait for him here."

"Not a bad idea at all," Sears grinned. "Well, Steve, now that you've cleaned up this mess for us, what are your plans?"

"I haven't any."

"How about taking bombers over to England for us as originally planned?" Sears asked. "Of course, it will be pretty tame after this."

"I'd like to," Steve declared. "And maybe it won't be so tame after all."

Although he could not know it, Steve's prophesy turned out to be truer than he dreamed as he was to learn later when he encountered the Phantom Battleship.

But, at the moment, all he could think of was that Chambert's plans had been defeated and his gang rounded up. He waited happily as Lieutenant Brown led Chambert to where he and Major Jeff Sears stood.

THE AIR COMBAT STORIES
for Boys

The record of daredevil exploits of these army and navy fliers over the front makes breathless reading. Their adventures have the ring of truth for both authors take them from their own rich experiences as wartime aviators.

DAREDEVILS OF THE AIR by Thomson Burtis

Recounts Lieutenant Riley's adventures as leader of The Phantom Five against the enemy in the air.

FOUR ACES by Thomson Burtis

As commanding officer of Special Flight A, Rud Riley and Jerry Lacey are thrown into the thickest of the air fighting.

WING FOR WING by Thomson Burtis

Continues the record of the daredevil young airman's adventures as one of the leading aces in the war.

FLYING BLACK BIRDS by Thomson Burtis

Stormy Lake leads a squadron of picked daredevils called the Black Birds against the famous German Red Devils.

DOOMED DEMONS by Eustace L. Adams

Ensign Jimmy Deal and his pals are reckless, carefree and fearless and their daredevil exploits make a swift, thrilling tale.

WINGS OF THE NAVY by Eustace L. Adams

Irrepressible Jimmy and his pal Pooch Mallory, assigned duty as observers on blimps, get into many scrapes — until they capture a German spy.

WAR WINGS by Eustace L. Adams

Jimmy gets in as tight a spot as air combat can provide when he tries to land on his own field in a captured Boche plane.

GROSSET & DUNLAP

Publishers   NEW YORK

THE X BAR X
Western Stories for Boys
by James Cody Ferris

The Manley boys, Roy and Teddy, are the sons of an old ranchman on the Great Plains, who owns many thousands of heads of cattle. The X-Bar-X punchers are real cowboys, but they're full of fun, too. Roy and Teddy can ride and shoot with the best of them, and manage to rope in more than their share of thrills and adventure.

THE X BAR X BOYS ON THE RANCH
IN THUNDER CANYON
ON WHIRLPOOL RIVER
ON BIG BISON TRAIL
AT THE ROUND-UP
AT NUGGET CAMP
AT RUSTLER'S GAP
AT GRIZZLY PASS
LOST IN THE ROCKIES
RIDING FOR LIFE
IN SMOKY VALLEY
AT COPPERHEAD GULCH
BRANDING THE WILD HERD
THE STRANGE RODEO
WITH THE SECRET RANGERS
HUNTING THE PRIZE MUSTANGS
AT TRIANGLE MINE
THE SAGEBRUSH MYSTERY
IN THE HAUNTED GULLY

GROSSET & DUNLAP

Publishers   NEW YORK

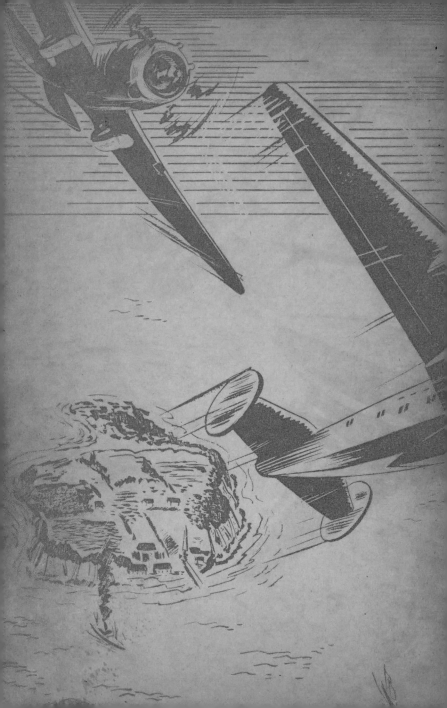